Jubilee

VIC KERRY

To Jim Green.

Chapter One

The Wasp unwrapped a disk of peppermint candy. The crinkling of the clear cellophane wrapper was no match for the muffled screams of the tweaker he'd picked up at the Flying J with the promise of methamphetamine for sex. She would get no drugs, but he would give her plenty of sex—rough, angry sex.

A dirty sock, something he'd taken off his last meth whore, hung from the girl's mouth like an argyle tongue. She looked like some kind of strange clown with the red splotches on her face and streaks of mascara. At that moment, the Wasp thought of her as the headlining act in his three-ring circus: kidnapping, rape and murder. It gave him a jolt of exhilaration as he thought about it. Lately, his lust for carnage made him sloppy. He'd almost gotten caught on the far side of Fort Smith, Arkansas. Fortunately, the Okie rubes they had for deputies couldn't have caught a cold sore at a herpes convention. If he was honest with himself, luck had been the reason he'd gotten away.

The Wasp took a large knife from the duffle bag and brandished it in front of the girl. She screamed louder and then whimpered. He loved that part of the show, the center ring drama of a tightrope act without a net—the part some folks watched through parted fingers, hoping the acrobat made it across, but secretly wanting to see him fall as well. The terror in his victim's eyes gave him almost as much satisfaction as the act of killing.

A sudden realization came to him as he reveled in the moment. The peppermint he'd stripped nude still rested in his hand. He'd almost forgotten to put it in his mouth. The rush of killing was so much better while sucking on the effervescent candy. He put the treat in his mouth.

The cool rush of mint sent a chill shivering through him. The first cut at the edge of the girl's mouth went all the way to her ear and prolonged that feeling. When he finished the Glasgow smile, the Wasp raped the girl, making sure the rubber he'd put on back at the truck stop stayed on during the struggle. He went to great lengths to keep as much DNA off his victims as possible. Although his interaction with the legal system had been limited, he'd shaved his body to prevent stray hairs from falling on the body of his victims. He kept the hair on his head closely cropped too.

Once the peppermint in his mouth melted into a sweet and minty memory, he finished off his victim with a quick slash across her throat. After all the high-flying anxiety of the trapeze act, the audience got to see the plummet to the ground. The rush of it sent shivers throughout his body.

The girl's corpse lay in a pool of her own deep, red blood. The argyle sock was so soaked in the stuff it resembled a real swollen tongue. Her eyes stared at him, and her knife-whittled smile grinned. He took another mint from his pocket, unwrapped it, and shoved it into her rectum as far as he could push it.

The Wasp went back to his stolen car and headed for the interstate.

Chapter Two

Vincent Price Green sat in his car looking at a ruby ring on his right hand. To anyone on the street, it would look like a class ring, but to him, it meant much more than that. The ring slid on his finger nowadays. He'd lost a lot of weight since he'd bought it on his daughter's 16th birthday. A lot of stuff had happened since then. Now the only thing that seemed to keep her real in his mind was that ring. Vince had been chasing her across the country for over a year, and Tulsa might be the end.

He always knew that he was a broken car part away from losing his daughter's track forever. His car would barely go. He'd taken it to the cheapest shop in town, where he got an estimate of a little over a thousand dollars. The ring on his finger wouldn't bring in that much money. The only thing he owned that would was the car. The title loan place was his last hope. During his travels, he'd had to pawn a lot of stuff to keep going. When his life's savings ran out a few months ago, this became a regular event. It left him with little more than the clothes on his back and his old beater. Now it was time to make the car work for him, too.

The air seemed too humid when he stepped out on the pavement. Dark clouds built up from the northeast. The sound of distant thunder rumbled above the sound of traffic on the busy street. A diesel truck growled by, hitting its jake brakes to add to the clamor. The man at the garage told him that they could have his car fixed in a day. He would have to spend one more night in Oklahoma. That would put him only a few days behind his daughter and her roving band of Gypsies.

On the last call he got from her, she said they were heading southeast across Alabama on Interstate 22. If they kept heading in that direction, they'd have to stop eventually. He doubted they would stow away on a ship when they hit the Atlantic Ocean. When they made it to the coast, he'd catch up with them. His daughter would call before then to check in. He worried a little that she hadn't already. Usually only three days passed between calls. Today marked the fourth day.

The rush of cold air focused Vince on his current mission. The title pawn shop smelled like a bank. This surprised him. He'd expected it to smell like the usual pawn shops he ended up in, a dusty perfume of old junk and gun oil. The employees looked different as well. A young man stood behind a counter, smiling and wearing a blue button-down shirt with a red tie emblazoned with the company's logo.

"Can I help you?" the man asked.

Vince walked to the counter and looked at the fellow's name tag. It read: Sterling. He smiled at him, with a smile that said he knew Sterling made a living off people so down on their luck that they had to beg for a small amount of cash for their most expensive possession. It was contemptuous not genial.

"I would like to pawn my car title," Vince pulled the title from his pocket and placed it on the counter.

Sterling picked it up and read the document. He looked at Vince and then past him at the car in the parking lot. "Is that it out there?"

"Yes, sir."

"Mileage?"

"Pushing 200,000 miles."

"200,000 miles? What, are you a traveling salesmen?" Sterling asked, sounding both jovial and sarcastic at the same time.

"To be honest with you, Sterling—may I call you that?" The title pawnbroker nodded. "Sterling, I'm chasing after my daughter. She's been gone for nearly two years following a jam band with a group of drugged-up hippies. I've run through my savings and now I'm broke."

"So you need to pawn your car title?" Sterling said. "I don't know if I'll be able to help you."

"Why not?"

"You're a bit of a flight risk," he said. "You told me that you're chasing your daughter around the country. That means you're not going to stay in Tulsa for long, and you don't have a permanent address."

"I'm good for it. It won't be much longer until I've caught up with her. Then I'll come back through and pay every dime back with the owed interest," Vince said.

"I've heard that before, Mr. Green. The problem is when you don't pay the money back, which you won't, I've got no collateral to collect on. You'll be in Maine or Timbuktu. Guess who'll be holding check?"

"You."

"Me. We can't help you. I'm sorry." Sterling pointed at the ring. "You could probably get quite a lot for that ring."

Vince pulled his hand to his chest and covered the ring with his hand as if protecting something precious, because he was. "I can't do that. This is the only real link I still have with my daughter."

"I guess you are stuck," Sterling said.

"Please, you have to help me, or I lose her forever. Do you have a daughter?"

"No," Sterling said.

"If you did and she ran off, wouldn't you do anything to get her back?"

"Probably." Sterling looked a little perturbed by Vince's behavior. He waved him close to the desk. "I don't know why I'm telling you this, because I don't get any kickbacks from it, but there is someone who can help you two stores down. It looks like a pizza place, and they make a fine pie, but they also make some fine loans."

"A loan shark?" Vince asked.

"Shhh. If my boss hears you, I'm sunk. Go over there and talk to them. If you make a deal, tell them Sterling sent you."

"I thought you said that you didn't get a kickback."

"I don't, but I do get a free pizza."

Vince walked back into the sticky air and building storm. For no longer than he'd been in the title loan place, the dark clouds had blown closer. Now they appeared overhead. He saw lightning flash inside them. A few fat drops of rain hit him as he walked down the sidewalk to the pizzeria. The smell of marinara sauce and garlic hit him before he opened the door. Once inside, the warmth of the place and the aroma of pizza almost overwhelmed him. A pretty woman stood behind the counter next to the cash register. He walked up to it.

"Did you call in an order?" she asked.

"No," Vince said. "Sterling from the title loan place sent me up here."

"Sterling?" she asked.

When he nodded his head, she smiled. He saw a gold-capped tooth on the bottom row near the back. She rang a small bell next to the cash register. A man with a greasy apron covering his greasy white pants and shirt walked from the back area. He held a cleaver in his hand. Vince wasn't quite sure why they needed a cleaver at a pizza shop.

"Sterling sent him. Get the boss," she said to the cook. When she turned back to Vince, her smile still beamed at him. "Larry will be up in a minute. Can I interest you in a slice of the daily special?"

"What is it?"

"Chicken and spinach with alfredo sauce," she said.

"No, thank you."

"No one ever wants the chicken spinach alfredo," said a deep voice with a long drawl, coming from the back.

Vince looked to see a man with white hair and a broad mustache walking toward him. The man wore a black Stetson hat and a gray cowboy-cut suit with a large belt buckle gleaming in the light. His cowboy boots clicked on the floor.

"This is Larry," the woman said.

"Larry Canada," the man said holding out his hand.

Vince shook it. The palm felt hard and callused from years of hard labor. Larry looked like a matinee cowboy, but his hands felt like he might have been the real deal at some point.

"I'm Vincent Green."

"Nice to meet you. I understand that my good pal Sterling sent you up here to see me."

"Yes, sir."

Larry laughed a gruff, husky-sounding laugh and slapped Vince on the back. "No need for the *sirs*. I'm Larry, and you're Vince. Let's see if we can get down to some business."

They walked to a booth at the back of the pizzeria. Larry sat so that he could see the door. This left Vince sitting with his back to it. He didn't like that arrangement too much, but he needed the money worse than the peace of mind. Larry scratched the side of his face before looking deeply into Vince's eyes.

"How old are you, Vince?" he asked.

"47," Vince answered.

"Looking at you, I'd guessed about 200, but what do I know. I'm some yahoo from Tulsa. What's aged you so much, Vince?"

"Is this how this kind of thing usually goes down?" Vince asked.

"What kind of a *thing* is going down?"

"Loan shark negotiations."

Larry rubbed his face again. This time it made him look a little like Lee Van Cleef in an old western right before he shot a man down. It made Vince uncomfortable. He needed this guy to stay happy.

"We don't call ourselves that," Larry said. "We prefer *no credit lenders*."

"I understand."

"Good. Now tell me what it is that makes you look so old," Larry said. "Rapport. It's good customer service."

"My daughter ran away. I've been chasing her, and I've run out of money."

"How much you need?"

"About $1,200."

"Collateral?"

"My car." Vince put the title on the table.

"It's kind of old. How many miles?"

"200,000. I'm not going to lie to you, Larry. I need that money."

"Now, exactly how am I going to get my property if you

don't pay me back?" Larry asked.

"I've recently gotten a job here in Tulsa for H&R Block. I'm an accountant. I don't get paid for a couple of weeks. My daughter is in Oklahoma City. I need the money to get her back and pay for a place to stay until I get my first paycheck."

"Address of this H&R Block location?"

Vince handed Larry a slip of paper with the address of the garage where he was taking his car. He'd written it down to help find the place. Larry took it and nodded his head. Then he took the title as well.

"We've got a deal—$1,200 to be paid back in one month's time with interest of 10 percent per day. Sound fair?"

"No," Vince said, "but I've got no choice."

"No, you don't," Larry said. "Tell Lucy at the counter to give you the money. *Pepperoni* is the password."

Vince nodded his head and left the booth as quickly as he could. The cashier gave him the money she'd put into a white sack with the pizzeria's logo on it. He took it and hurried out of the place. His next stop would be the garage if his car could hold out that long.

Chapter Three

A redhead with obvious herpes sores on her face smoked a cigarette beside the Flying J's side entrance. The Wasp had seen his fair share of lot lizards, but this one needed to molt if she expected to get a john. He felt like the least he could do was to put the poor thing out of her misery. The last thing he'd ever want was to get stuck in Oklahoma with no way or hope of getting to some place better. The burning urge to kill hadn't overtaken him yet. With a fresh kill a day before, that sensation would still be days away. This one would be for fun . He walked over to her.

"You got another one of those smokes?" he asked.

She looked him up and down as if trying to size him up—something the Wasp didn't get much from women. Occasionally some smart aleck guy would try and start something, and he would usually get quite a shock when the Wasp lit into him. He may look average in size and to some even a little weak, but the Wasp packed a punch, and he knew it. No matter how large or small, the sting of a wasp always hurt. The delightfully skanky redhead smiled at him. He saw the black holes eaten into the top of her front teeth. Like an everlasting gobstopper, her every layer brought some new surprise.

"Sure," she pulled a crushed pack of cheap cigarettes out of her back pocket. "Help yourself."

He took one and felt hesitant to put the thing to his lips. If the woman's face looked like an oozing pepperoni pizza, the Wasp could only imagine how her nether regions looked. This would be one victim who would remain clothed and possibly free from his trademark calling card, unless he still had some latex surgical gloves in the console of his car. If he was going to make the transaction, smoking the cigarette was necessary. He put it between his lips and used his own Bic to light it. The taste of the cheap tobacco almost made him retch. He never could figure how anyone could smoke such cheap stuff. When you looked like the redhead, the price of cigarettes probably didn't matter too much. Her drug of choice was methamphetamine. By the looks of her, she'd been living off it for a while.

"You waiting for a ride?" he asked.

"Always. You offering?"

"If you need one, I'm heading toward Arkansas," the Wasp said. "I could always use the company."

"I was hoping for Dallas, but anywhere is better than here."

The Wasp dropped his cigarette on the ground and stubbed it out with his foot. He motioned for her to do the same. His car would hold her stench longer than he would like, but the smell of cheap cigarettes would take even longer to air out.

They got into his stolen silver-tone Toyota Camry, which looked like every third or fourth car on the road, and he made his way back to the interstate. The woman talked nonstop. The Wasp didn't listen. She had nothing that interested him even if she weren't a mercy kill. He came up to the next exit after about four miles. It looked lonely, like an exit that went to a rural road with no town within a five-mile stretch. No lamps lit the way. It was the perfect place to end the redhead's hitching days.

"Why are we getting off here?" she asked.

"End of the road," the Wasp said.

"I thought you were going to Arkansas?"

"I am, but you're not."

He smiled at her. In the light of the dashboard instruments, he saw her face become locked with terror. As soon as the car slowed enough, the woman bailed. The Wasp liked it when they did that. He brought the car to a stop and jumped out. The redhead was too strung out to do much effective running. She zigzagged but stumbled with every other step. He caught her without breaking a sweat.

"Why are you running?" he asked.

"You're going to kill me," she said, stumbling to the ground like some victim in a slasher movie.

The Wasp laughed at her answer and her fall. "Of course I am, but running wouldn't help you."

He reached behind him and took a hunting knife from a sheath at the small of his back. The redhead screamed, but the noise from a big rig on the interstate swallowed it up. The blade slashed across her throat. The scent of her hot blood perfumed the air. Her scream garbled to nothing. The Wasp watched the life fade out of her eyes. Whatever drug she was on pushed the blood through her body so hard that she bled out faster than anyone he'd ever killed. He finished his job by giving her some good slices across the face. To his delight, he found there was a glove in the console. A peppermint in her rectum would be the *piece de resistance*. The last thing the Wasp wanted to do was leave a victim without the police knowing it was him. Two murders in a row would give the criminologist something to think about. He'd never done that before.

The night still felt young as he smoked one of his good cigarettes and savored the kill. He would put some miles on the road before turning in for the night. It would be best to get some space between him and the scene of the crime.

Chapter Four

Vince stared at the ceiling of his motel room. It was the kind of place a guy would check-in to commit suicide. The wallpaper clung to the walls with the aid of Scotch tape. The television sat on a three-drawer dresser with peeling veneer. It had dials for channel selection. Although the sign under the neon Indian chopping with his tomahawk read HBO, Vince doubted the TV got more than NBC on a good night.

The room cost next to nothing, which is what he had left in his wallet. Only his ring was left to pawn. He'd sell himself before that ring.

As he tried to sleep with the smell of dead bugs perfuming the air, Vince's mind wandered. He thought about where Sara Beth might be. This led his mind back to his poor situation. The ring weighed his finger down as if suddenly turned into lead — the reverse alchemy of regret. Finally his mind took a tangential jag to Nashville, Tennessee. The memory played out like a movie. It almost flickered.

Vince had surprised Sara Beth with the trip to the Music City for her 16th birthday. Back then, the girl was crazy for country music. The twangy voice of a Southern boy filled her with giddiness. She would smile every time a Kenny Chesney song played on the radio.

Second Avenue thumped with music poured out from the neon-lit honky-tonks. The warm Southern air bore a humidity that Vince had never felt. California never felt that way. He liked it. Sara Beth commented on it too.

"We've got enough time to eat before the show," he said as they stood on the corner by the Bridgestone Arena. "What do you want?"

"I guess sushi isn't an option," she said.

"Probably not," he replied. "That's more of a Cali thing."

"So what's a Tennessee thang?" she asked, faking a bad

Southern accent.

"Collard greens," Vince said.

"What are those?"

"I'm not sure. I heard them mentioned in Southern movies. You want to find some?"

"No." Sara Beth sounded like the 16-year-old she was instead of using her I-think-I'm-grown tone.

A couple passed them. They each wore Titans t-shirts. Vince figured they were locals. He stopped them. True to the form that he'd experienced since arriving in Tennessee, they were polite.

"Yes, sir, what can I do for you?" the man asked.

"This is our first time in town," Vince said.

"Welcome," the woman said. "Sounds like you came from a ways off."

"Los Angeles," Sara Beth said. "It's my 16th birthday present."

"That's sweet," the woman said. "A sweet, sweet 16."

Sara Beth smiled. It was her polite one she gave when she found people *too much*. The hokiness in the woman's speech gave Vince a bit of a toothache too, but it sounded sincere.

"So what was it you needed help with?" the man asked to refocus the conversation.

"We don't know what or where to eat," Vince said.

"Not much sushi around here, is there?" the woman said. "That's something y'all Californians like to eat, isn't it?"

"We do," Sara Beth answered, still smiling her big fake smile.

"I'd suggest barbeque," the man said. "We got plenty of places that serve it, and you really can't beat it."

Vince looked at his daughter. "How about it?"

"Sounds heavy," she said.

"It's a long walk back to the hotel. We can burn some of it off after the concert."

She nodded. "Okay."

He turned back to the couple who patiently waited for them to finish their conversation. "Where's the best place close by? We're going to the Grand Ole Opry at the Ryman tonight, so I don't want to wander too far."

"Jack's is right over yonder," the man said. "Some of the best food in the city."

"Thanks," Vince said.

The couple walked past them. Vince and Sara Beth ate at Jack's. They loved it. She said if they moved to the South that she would gain 100 pounds from barbeque alone. They went to the show. Kenny Chesney wasn't in the lineup, but George Strait was. Sara Beth liked him too, even if he was an "old guy." The highlight was a surprise performance by Dolly Parton. She sang "I Will Always Love You." Vince took the opportunity to give Sara Beth her ruby necklace, which was the final part of his present. She cried when he showed her his ring that matched it. He told her that those two pieces of jewelry would represent their undying bond as father and daughter.

His thoughts brought him back full circle to the present. He still stared at the ceiling in the depressing room. The air conditioner clicked on. The fan rattled. A strong odor of old cigarette smoke came with the cooler air. The night would be miserable. Vince thought he might be better off sleeping in his car. It smelled bad too, but he'd spent so much time in it, he hardly noticed anymore. The charger plug in his car didn't work, and he needed to charge his phone. If it was dead when Sara Beth called, he might lose track of her for good.

His mind wandered again. This time to nothing in particular. His fifth birthday party came up followed by a joke from *Smokey and the Bandit*. Brains worked that way, following random rabbits down their holes. Sleep approached as his thoughts became more abstract with a pleasant cotton-stuffed quality. His eyelids lay heavy. The ceiling faded into the gauzy vision of pre-slumber.

His phone rang with its loud old-timey telephone ringtone. It jarred him from his doze. Everything crashed around him as a start echoed down his body. Vince snatched his phone from the bedside table. The charging cable popped off and clattered across the tabletop. A strange number from the 205 area code scrolled across the screen. He had no idea where the call was coming from but hoped it was his daughter.

"Hello," he almost yelled into the receiver.

"Daddy," Sara Beth's voice sounded like water to a man in the Sahara.

"Baby, it's good to hear your voice," Vince almost laughed with delight. "Where are you?"

"On a pay phone."

"They still have those?"

"They do here," she said.

"Where's here, baby? Where are you?"

"A little town called Jubilee in Alabama. Daddy, I can't talk for long. I only had a couple of quarters."

"Go on."

"I think I want to come home. Can I?"

"Can you?" He couldn't hide his joy. "Of course you can. Why do you think I've been chasing you all over creation? I've wanted you back since the moment you left."

"I didn't know if you might have changed your mind. You've lost everything because of me," she said.

"You are the only thing I need. You are my everything."

"Daddy, can you come and get me?"

"I can be there soon. My car isn't in the best shape. I can only drive about an hour before I have to stop and let it cool off."

"They're leaving tomorrow. Woodchuck won't let me stay behind."

"Remember what I told you," Vince said. "Hide out at the Salvation Army."

"I don't think this town has one," she said. "We've been shacked up at an old—"

"I'm sorry, but the time has expired," a computerized voice broke into the conversation.

"No!" Vince screamed.

The phone fell from his hand and slid under the bed. He fumbled to find it. When he recalled the number, it rang, but no one picked up. She must have left when her money ran out. He supposed she didn't know that someone could call back without it being charged.

Vince gathered his belongings and ran into the humid night air. His car was parked in front of his room door. He tossed his things into the back seat and crawled behind the steering wheel. His daughter needed him right then. He'd drive his car until it burst into flames if he had to.

The engine wouldn't turn over. Vince tried to crank it several times with the same results. Then he noticed that none of the lights came on. The battery was shot. Another expense he could not afford.

He got out of his car and slammed the door. No matter how desperately he needed to get to Sara Beth, it wasn't happening tonight. He'd have to figure something out. The motel was too far from a town to walk. He felt hope sliding away, but if Sara Beth took his advice, he might still get to her anyway.

Chapter Five

The Wasp sat on the guardrail by a dark road. His car straddled the center line, idling. He took a drag off a cigarette as he listened to the man in the driver seat scream until his voice cracked. The worse part of this whole plan was waiting for the adhesive to dry. The pimpled-face teen at Home Depot had told him that it was the strongest glue the store sold. Of course, it needed a period of time to cure. The guy he'd hitched a ride with from the truck stop had been screaming ever since he'd regained consciousness with his hands lashed to the steering wheel while his palms dried to the vinyl. The poor man didn't seem as concerned about his feet that were glued to the floorboard and gas pedal. The Wasp wished he'd drugged the dude to shut him up, but that wasn't his style.

The cherry on the cigarette burned to the filter. The Wasp flicked it onto the grass. It sizzled out in the dew. He thought how lucky it was that he happened up on this guy when he needed him the most. Except for their faces, they could be twins. Someone had gotten a look at him when he snatched the girl he'd killed the night before. The cops were looking for him and his car. The only option he had was to kill himself. No one had ever gotten a description of him before, and now the cops had a good one. It would be hard to go around without getting recognized, despite what a good chameleon he could be. The Wasp hated overly complicated disguises, so any kind of theatrical getup wasn't going to happen. Those things seemed too Hollywood. He'd left that place behind along with a string of dead junkies strewn along Hollywood Boulevard and the Sunset Strip, not to mention the ones littering the highways from the Golden State to Arkansas.

The stunt-double started screaming again. His voice sounded hoarser. The Wasp looked at his watch. The timer he'd set ticked down to a minute. The glue had enough time to set. That was a good thing because he couldn't take any more of the guy's caterwauling. He didn't mind listening to a woman scream. It helped get him off, but when a guy made that kind of noise, it put him off. Most of the time he'd whack a guy without any frills — no muss, no fuss. Killing a screaming man made him feel like he was cutting up Barry Gibb in the middle of his falsetto chorus to "Staying Alive." The Wasp loved the Bee Gees and hated the idea of doing that.

He walked around to the back of the car. The exhaust felt hot against his leg. He'd kept the car in neutral on the flat stretch of road. If anyone drove past, he'd tell them he was puking. If that didn't work, he would have to kill them and then simply carry on with his scheme. The cops would think it was one last murder before the end, because someone like him would certainly want to go out with a bang. That's what a criminologist would say.

The stunt double's voice broke again when the Wasp got to the driver's door. He opened it, and the man looked at him with pleading eyes.

"Don't kill me," he said with a raw voice. "I've got kids. I'll give you all my money."

"You already have," the Wasp said. "Remember, I took your wallet."

"I'll give you the PIN to my bank account."

The Wasp shook his head in disagreement. "That's a quick way to get caught. This whole thing is so that I can walk away scot-free."

"Please."

"Shut up, or I'm going to stick a pine cone up your ass," the Wasp reached in and pulled on the man's hand. The palms held fast to the steering wheel. "I'm not joking by the way. I never joke about rectal insertion."

The stunt-double stopped pleading. The Wasp unlashed his wrists from the steering column. He reached across the man and nudged the gearshift to drive. The road was so flat the car barely moved.

"What's your name?" the Wasp asked, straightening up and walking beside the slow rolling car.

"Jeff Henderson."

"You will not be forgotten Jeff Henderson. When you get to Hell, tell Satan the Wasp sent you."

He curled his fist and slammed it into Jeff Henderson's balls. The stunt double huffed, bent forward and flexed his legs. The engine revved. The car accelerated. The Wasp had quick enough reflexes to move before the door slammed against him or the tires rolled over his feet. He watched as Jeff Henderson tried to steer. The car never slowed as it started around a sharp curve. The sound of the metal and glass crunching when the car hit a tree gave the Wasp a giddy feeling in his stomach. His luck held out. He saw the orange flicker of flames. The car had caught fire, and the adhesive would melt away. The girlish screams of Jeff Henderson would no longer echo through the night. Since he'd used gasoline to cause the fire, the cops would think it was all part of the wreck. With his stunt double's remains charred to a crisp, the cops wouldn't realize that the Wasp was still alive until he had time to be several states away.

He walked up the road to where he had hidden Jeff's car. Lighting another cigarette, he got into the hatchback and drove into the night.

Chapter Six

When Vince slipped into the back pew, he knew that he must have come at the end of the services. The congregation was already singing "Night, with Ebon Pinion." A song leader beat time from the pulpit. Most everyone stood, and the minister paced between the front pews and the communion table. He was okay with that. The intention had never been to listen to a sermon. Too many Sundays of his youth had been spent dangling over the pits of Hell while a preacher extolled the preciousness of the grace of God that protected from all damnation.

The song ended, but the congregation continued to stand, so Vince did too. The man at the front said some pleasantries, including welcoming visitors. Vince figured he was the only visitor by the looks of the small number of people in the auditorium. A number was called out. Hymnal pages turned with the whooshing sound of pious parishioners readying themselves for a closing song. They began singing a tune he'd never heard. It was short, and after the last note, an old man who was barely audible prayed, or rather mumbled. Vince only knew the prayer ended when the people began to fill the aisle.

A man wearing a tan suit standing in front of Vince turned around with a broad smile and extended his right hand. Vince rubbed his hands on his jeans to make sure they weren't sweaty and shook it.

"I'm Bob Halston. It is nice to have you visit with us," the man said.

"Thank you. I'm Vincent Green."

"Are you from Jubilee or just passing through, Vincent?" Bob Halston asked, using his first name as if they had been old friends. Something in the man's jovial face told Vincent it was sincere and not a hypocritical greeting to keep up appearances.

"Kind of. I'm looking for someone," Vince said. "My daughter ran away a while ago. I'm tracking her down."

"We get a lot of traffic through this area because of the interstate," Bob said. "Problem is it's like trying to find the proverbial needle in a haystack."

Vince nodded and felt weary at that moment. "You don't have to tell me that. I've been weaving back and forth across a dozen states following leads, always a step behind."

"What makes you think that she came through our little town?" Bob said. "There's not much here to attract a runaway except the interstate."

"I got a call from her a few days ago. She told me she was here. I got delayed due to car trouble."

"I suppose you came to find solace with the Lord," Bob said. "Understandable."

Vince gave the man a wry grin. "Actually, I came here because I've learned along the way that women at church seem to know the most about the scuttlebutt in a town, and also aren't too tight with their lips."

Bob laughed a jovial laugh and slapped his thigh. "I've never heard it said like that, but you probably came to the right place." He turned and pointed to three elderly women near the front of the church. "Those are the Bellflower Sisters. If there is anyone in this church who would know if your daughter has come through these parts, they're it. They are the least tight lips in the whole community. Understand that I'm not gossiping, just relaying the truth."

"Thank you," Vince said.

"No problem. I wish you all the luck in the world, and I'm going to pray for you too." Bob patted him on the shoulder.

The sentiment made Vince feel hopeful. Many people along the way had promised to talk to the Lord for him, but Bob was the only one he really believed would do it. Something told him that if God existed Bob might be the only person He would answer.

Vince slipped out of the pew and headed up the aisle to the three women. They stood in a line from the shortest to the tallest. Each wore a matching dress of a different color. The shortest of the three appeared to be the youngest, with curly brown hair tinged with gray and a pug nose. The tallest was the oldest with a long nose, plenty of wrinkles on the loose skin of her fleshy face. Her hair was steel gray. The middle appeared to be just that: the middle sister. Her white hair shimmered almost silver, and she wore cat-eye glasses.

"Excuse me, are you the Bellflower sisters?" he asked as humbly as he could.

Each looked at him in succession, starting with the tallest. Their eyes studied him, bore into him. For the first time in a long time, Vince felt completely naked, vulnerable in the midst of them.

"Yes," they answered in sync.

"Jinx, you owe me a Coke," the tallest and shortest said.

"Enough of your silliness," the middle sister said, giving her sisters a look that told them to grow up. She turned back to Vince. "We are the Bellflower sisters. What do you need?"

"That gentleman, Bob Halston," he pointed to the older man, "said you might be able to help me."

"It's according," the tall sister said.

"I'm looking for someone," Vince said.

"You came to the right people," they said together again.

"Jinx, you owe me a Coke," the shortest and tallest announced.

"Who are you looking for?" the middle sister asked.

"My daughter." He took a creased photograph from his pocket and showed it to them.

"Have lunch with us," the tallest one said. "And we'll see what we can do."

Vince smiled and nodded his agreement. If eating with three eccentric old birds would find his daughter, he'd cook them a seven course meal and serve it on solid gold chargers.

During the interim from leaving the church to being seated at the local diner, Vince learned the Bellflower sisters' names. It made it a little easier for him to think about them.

The tallest and indeed the oldest of the sisters was named Lily

Bellflower-Owens. The middle sister in all ways was Camilla. The baby sister landed the name Petunia, but her sisters called her Tunie. She seemed the oddest of the three. Something about her seemed off, but he couldn't pinpoint what it was. She acted childlike in an intangible way.

The Bellflower sisters insisted on a booth. Vince found himself crammed against the window with Lily on the outside. Camilla sat across from him, and Tunie beside her.

"Can we talk about my daughter now?" he asked after the women came back from the salad bar, laden with everything on it that wasn't actually a vegetable.

"Of course," Tunie said. "What is her name?"

"Sara Elizabeth Green. Sometimes she goes by Sara, other times by Beth. Mostly she goes by Sara Beth."

"Let me see her picture again. I couldn't tell much at the church," Lily asked with a mouthful of macaroni salad.

Vince showed her the picture again. "Sara Beth has light brown hair with a fair complexion a sprinkle of freckles. She's about 19-years-old. This pic is a couple of years old."

"Looks like about every other girl," Camilla said. She pointed at a waitress. "Is that her?"

Vince felt cross at Camilla for making light of his situation. She gave him a bad taste in his mouth like indigestion.

"Of course that's not her. I wish you would be more serious. Sara Beth may be in danger or even dead. I know she was in this town. She told me herself."

"Was she alone?" Tunie asked.

"No, she was with a boy about 18 or 19. Ugly fellow. The last time I saw him he had this ponytail. He had a lot of freckles. His name was Woodchuck."

"Woodchuck," Lily said, like a bolt of lightning hit her.

Vince expected a smart comment from her, but instead she set her fork down and gave him her focused attention.

"He stayed with us for about three days," she said.

"Are you sure it's the guy I'm talking about?"

"How many people are called Woodchuck?" Lily asked. "A

girl was with him along with a couple of other guys. I don't remember her name. It was something made up sounding."

"Did she look like the picture?" he asked.

"Persephone," Camilla said. "Her name was Persephone, but she had short purple hair and looked sickly and pale. Looked like a vampire or something."

Vince nodded his head. "That sounds like her. She got into some weird stuff before following that stupid jam band. Is she still around?"

"No," Tunie said.

"Where did she go? Did she leave with Woodchuck?" Vince asked.

"I don't remember," Camilla said.

Camilla lied. Vince could tell. He'd seen a lot of people lie since he set out after his daughter. Camilla was good at it. She didn't have an obvious tell, but she was deceitful by nature. He thought it was like watching a snake.

"Neither do I," Tunie said. "I can't remember if she ever said."

Vince believed Tunie. The youngest one acted different from her sisters. She talked like a much younger person, like someone trapped in adolescence. He imagined that she might be mentally ill. If that were the case, she might not remember where or when his daughter left.

"I make everyone who stays with us leave a forwarding address before they leave, in case they forget something. It'll be in the book at the house," Lily said.

"Do you run a hotel?" Vince asked.

"A bed and breakfast," Lily said. "*Tunie* and I run it. We get a lot of people passing through our little town because of the interstate, but we don't have many affordable motels that anyone would want to stay at. We give travelers an option for longer stays if they need them."

"Or a free one," Camilla said with a bitter tone.

Lily stared at her sister but said nothing in response. The tension between them stretched so taut Vince thought he could pluck it like the string of guitar.

"Can we go look at that book?" Vince said, risking the wrath of the two ladies.

"Of course," Lily said.

"What if guests don't have a forwarding address?" Vince asked. "She's been on the lam for a while, drifting around."

"I make them at least give me a town," Lily said.

Vince almost couldn't eat because of his flurry of excitement, but he forced himself because it had been a while since he'd filled his belly with real food. Beef jerky and Chef Boyardee only satisfied for so long. The Bellflower sisters took their time. Every bite dragged out to an eternity. He felt like a gunslinger waiting for high noon to roll around. Finally, they swallowed the last morsel. He offered to pay for their lunch, but didn't have enough to pay for the whole meal. He slipped what he had into the receipt holder and ushered the old ladies out before the waitress took it away. Dine and ditch wasn't the worst thing he'd ever done. Getting the information to find his daughter eased his conscience about the trick. If he succeeded at getting Sara Beth back, he'd mail the place the difference with a little interest thrown in for good karmic measure.

Chapter Seven

Vince sat in the parlor of the Bellflower Inn. It felt uncomfortable. The antique furniture looked on the verge of being more like yard sale junk. The wallpaper was yellowed from years of exposure. A cuckoo clock ticked away. The sun shone through the windows and hit the back of his chair. It warmed the room too much. Beads of sweat formed at his hair line. The place felt like wearing a too tight sweater.

The old ladies' conversation buzzed from the room adjacent to the parlor. They had gone to look for the register book. He'd made the mistake of thinking they would have been organized. The cuckoo popped out of the clock and told him a different story. The sisters had been searching for at least fifteen minutes. At any moment the hour would be reached, and the bird would sing again.

Vince hated cuckoo clocks. They reminded him of his grandmother. She had been a strange old lady from the old country. A clock similar to the one at the Bellflower Inn had maddeningly ticked and cuckooed in her living room, which also had worn-out pieces of furniture and dirty wallpaper. She would tell him tales about how if he didn't behave, the cuckoo bird would come alive and peck his eyes out. Every time that thing chimed, little boy Vince would lose his mind, and his grandmother would laugh.

He remembered her like the old witch who lived in the gingerbread house. His grandmother hardly ever went without a lit cigarette in her mouth. One day while she cleaned her stove with a highly flammable chemical, her luck ran out. The fumes ignited. The rush of flames caught her heavily sprayed bouffant and polyester nightgown on fire. She burned up like the old witch in *Hansel and Gretel*.

The hour mark passed, and the dread bird cuckooed. It shot a bolt of fear through him. A little part of him expected his scorched grandmother's corpse to come in from the other room cackling at his sudden terror.

"We found it," Lily said, walking into the room.

For a moment, Vince thought his horrifying daydream had come true. The spiral bounded notebook with a pink cartoon cat smiling from the cover brought him back to the stark reality of his situation. His grandmother rotted in the ground in California, and his daughter was on the run.

Vince had expected something more formal than a child's notebook. He didn't know why, after he'd been sitting and observing for so long. The old ladies must be living on a shoestring budget. No wonder they had no problem with him buying their lunch. The lingering memory of his evil grandmother faded away into sympathy for the sisters.

"Do you have her destination written in it?" he asked.

"Haven't looked yet," Lily said, "but I don't let anyone go without leaving it."

She opened the book and flipped the lined pages until she found the entry. Her crooked, arthritic finger scanned down the page. She nodded and tapped the place where she'd found the name.

"It says here that Persephone Song left on the twelfth. Said she was heading to Nashville."

"Nashville. Did she specify a location?"

"That's all my book says," Lily held the notebook out to him.

Vince took it from her. The handwriting was shaky and hard to read, but he'd seen worse. Sure enough, Persephone Song listed herself as heading to Nashville. There was no definite address. He hoped Sara Beth took his advice and headed to a shelter. It would be easier to find her that way. Although her track record for listening to him wasn't very good, she'd sounded so tired on the phone when she called him. He thought that this time she might listen to him.

Vince looked at the remaining names in the book. A different scratchy handwriting showed that Woodchuck had left a day later for Miami. He tucked that away in his memory in case he needed it.

"Woodchuck left after Sara Beth," he said. "He was heading to Miami. Do you know if he tried to hassle her to go with him?"

"I don't know. I don't remember Persephone leaving at all." Lily took the notebook and stared at the handwriting. "I didn't log her in. Camilla did. She might know."

"Please find out," Vince said.

"Camilla, come in here a minute," Lily yelled.

The middle sister walked in wiping her hands on an apron. She looked a little put out. "What is it? I've got sugar melting on the stove. I left Tunie stirring it. Lord knows how that might turn out. The other day, I had her help me make peppermint taffy. She dyed her pieces red. They're supposed to be red and white striped. I can't sell them like that. I'll have to give them away."

Lily showed her the book. "Do you remember if that Woodchuck character gave Persephone a hard time about not going with him to Miami?"

"She left in the middle of the night while he was passed out upstairs," Camilla said. "She asked me how far Nashville was from here. I told her. She looked ecstatic when she left."

Vince studied Camilla's eyes while she answered the question. She hid something from them. He didn't trust the middle sister very much. She was not as friendly as her sisters. Anyone else might not notice it, but it was true. Camilla forced niceness at times. It showed in her smile that lacked ease.

"Get back in here," Tunie called from where Vince assumed was the kitchen. "I think this stuff is about to boil over."

Camilla hurried out of the room. Lily closed the book and gave Vince a look that told him she hoped that helped.

"I need to get to Nashville," he said.

Reality hit him. His car ran on fumes. There was no way he was going anywhere with an empty wallet.

"I thought you were out of money," Lily said.

"I am. If I opened my wallet in a cartoon, moths would flutter out."

"If you help around here, I can give you a room for a few

days. Maybe you could work odd jobs in town for a little money," Lily said. "Camilla has been needing a hand down at the candy shop. You heard how it's been going using Tunie as help. She might give you some money to do that."

"So, you have income besides what this place brings in?" Vince asked.

"A little bit," Lily said.

"Do you think you could advance me enough for gas to get to Nashville? I don't want to miss her. I realize it's a big thing to ask, seeing as how we just met."

"I don't know. It's *our* money. I'll have to ask my sisters."

With that, Lily left him sitting in the parlor, staring at the yellowing wallpaper again. Fortunately, the cuckoo wouldn't pop out for another forty-five minutes.

***

Lily joined her sisters in the kitchen as Camilla stirred her pot of boiling sugar. A candy thermometer stuck up from the sauce pan. Tunie sat on a stool beside Camilla and watched. She swung her legs absent-mindedly like a lovestruck teenager staring at the poster of a matinee idol. She seemed to be doing that a lot more lately.

"What is it?" Camilla asked.

Lily stepped closer to her sisters so that she could whisper. "I needed to run something past you girls without our guest hearing us."

"What is it?" Tunie asked.

"He wants us to give him some money so that he can get his daughter in Nashville," Lily said.

"No," Camilla said. "We're not the First National Bank."

"I offered for him to work for us, but he stated he needed it quickly. He's afraid that he might lose her trail," Lily said. "Maybe, we can get him to sign an agreement to come back and work it off when he finds her."

"I stand by what I said," Camilla said.

"What about his daughter?" Lily said. "That girl was sweet. I'd hate to think about her living on the streets up in Nashville.

29

There's no telling what might happen to her."

"We don't even know if he has a daughter," Camilla said. "He gives me the creeps. You remember the news report about that raping serial killer. He might be him."

Camilla picked up some oven mitts and lifted her boiling pot off the stove eye. She poured in some peppermint oil and stirred it. The room quickly filled with the smell of the confection.

Lily thought her sister made the best candies around. Most other people in town thought the same. Camilla's candy shop was the only thing that kept the sisters in consistent money. Lately it hadn't been enough.

"But he had a picture of Persephone," Tunie said.

"He called his daughter *Sara Beth*," Camilla said, pouring some of the liquid sugar into a bowl. "The picture looked like a million girls. Remember that Persephone Song had short purple hair. The girl in that picture had much longer hair and didn't look as if she'd been ridden hard and put away wet."

"Why would he stick to the story so adamantly?" Lily asked. She wanted to help him. It felt like the scripture about not feeding or clothing Jesus might be coming true, but she could do nothing without her sister's blessings. Their money was too limited to act alone.

"Crooks are like that." Camilla colored one bowl of the sugar red.

"The Bible says that we may have hosted angels unawares," Tunie said.

"It also says, 'Thou shalt not steal,'" Camilla said. "He didn't pay the bill at lunch. We'll have to go back and take care of it."

Lily had noticed that Vince ditched on the bill. She'd hoped that her sisters hadn't. Camilla seemed to be against giving him anything. Lily would have to press the right buttons. She knew what would pull her sister's heartstring.

"What about that killer?" Lily said.

Camilla jerked her head around. A shocked expression faded from her face. "What do you mean?"

"They found a dead girl in Arkansas with a peppermint up

inside her," Tunie said. "That could happen to his daughter."

Camilla turned back to her candy. "I'll say it again. As far as we know, he could be the killer."

"Let's give him some money to find his daughter. He's away from his family. She's alone. He's alone. What if you were alone and needed help, Camilla?" Lily said. "What would you do?"

"I'd want help," Camilla said.

"You would be at the mercy of the kindness or hardheartedness of strangers," Lily said.

Camilla's eyes softened and looked thoughtful. Lily thought she glimpsed tears welling up.

"Fine," Camilla said. "Fifty dollars is enough for gas, and see if you can get him to come back and work it off."

Lily took Vince the money and wished him luck without bothering to ask him for payback. He wasted no time leaving. As she watched him drive away, she wondered if he was the highway killer the news called the Peppermint Slasher. If so, the sisters had lucked up by not being his victims.

Finally, as she sat on the big porch swing and swayed in the afternoon breeze, she thought about the money he took with him. Three final notices on bills sat on the desk in her office. Alabama Power threatened to cut them off in two weeks. The cable company already had. It didn't help business at a bed and breakfast to not offer cable television. Few people thought much of a well-stocked library of classics and romance novels. The notice that scared her most was the mortgage. They might lose the place. Hopefully, when the fair came to town in a few weeks, Camilla would be able to make lots of money in her midway booth. Usually, she brought in a small fortune from the sales. She'd pulled them from the fire in the past by selling candy and caramel apples.

Chapter Eight

The Wasp sat in Wendy's watching the customers. He ate his spicy chicken sandwich with much care, savoring every single flavor. If anyone was watching him, they'd think he was some kind of fast food connoisseur, a critic maybe. The atmosphere of the place made him tingle. So many people milled around him not realizing that any one of them could be his next victim. That idea aroused and excited him. The urge to kill was always present. It was part of his personality. As he savored another bite of his sandwich mingled with the saltiness of ketchup, he thought the desire was more than that. Killing was part of his essence, his soul. Not being able to kill was like not having an arm.

The police were currently operating under the belief that he had died in a fiery car crash back near the Oklahoma state line. The last thing he needed was to pick up the attractive hitchhiker with pink hair who sat a few booths away. She needed to die. Everything about her told him she was the perfect victim. No one would look for her for a long time. The body might never be identified. Thinking about taking everything away from a person made him feel like he might come, right there in a freaking Wendy's.

He turned his attention to his sandwich. He crammed his mouth with another large bite along with another wad of fries slathered in ketchup. Some of the sauce hit the foil paper like a drop of blood. For the first time, he felt trapped. Wendy's didn't give him that feeling; the whole city of Memphis did. He wouldn't have to be there if his *sister* hadn't run out on him. They had been the perfect team. She would lure in the victims with her innocent WASP features. He'd do the deed while she made sure to get any valuables. His sister watched everything he did. She learned everything there was to learn about the art of killing. She bolted on him, taking most of his money and worse, knowing his identity.

The Wasp finished his sandwich. He took his tray, threw away the garbage, and left the restaurant that exited into the convenience store part of the truck stop. It bustled as much as Wendy's had. More truckers milled around the place than families. The urge to kill tamped down a bit in this part of the place. He rarely killed men. As he looked at the case of books on CD, he knew that was a lie. Occasionally one of his victims would be a man, but always a certain type. The Wasp would never try to take on one of the road-savvy truckers. They had a lot of fight in them. Most of them were addicts to amphetamines or booze. A trucker hopped up on Ritalin wasn't a target easily taken down. Although the thrill of a hard kill was always the ultimate sexual feeling, getting hurt—or worse, getting caught biting off more than he could chew—wasn't.

The cover of a book on CD caught his attention. It depicted a girl blindfolded, looking both bloodied and sexy at the same time. The Wasp wasn't the literary sort. He'd read in the past when he swindled old ladies. That was before he got into the hardcore killing. The old ladies loved those stupid cozy mysteries and poetry. Keats and Shakespeare had been the final things some of those geriatrics heard as he smothered them with a pillow. *Shall I compare thee to a summer's day?* The illustration on the cover reminded him of his *sister*. He'd like to make her look like that, beaten but beautiful. The Wasp grabbed the case. He checked out, buying *The Girl Next Door* by a guy named Jack Ketchum. It was steal at only $5.

The air outside the Love's Truck Stop felt sticky and a little too warm for the time of the year. A storm brewed. He saw flashes of lightning to the west. Back across the Mississippi River, probably not far into Arkansas, the thunderstorm wreaked havoc on the population. Hail would be in the storm and maybe even a tornado. He decided to head across the street to his motel. The book on CD would have to wait until tomorrow, when he would head out for a new place to flop.

Memphis would be his home for a little longer. His sister might be hiding somewhere in the city. She was probably passed out in some crack house or at the Salvation Army. He'd taught her about the shelters, not the drug dens. There was only one thing the Wasp practiced without fail, and that was abstinence from drugs. Killing was the best high he could ever achieve. He'd tried to teach his sister that, just like he had all the sisters before her. Only one of them ever understood that but she'd been stupid, and the cops in San Jose took care of her. The others he'd had to handle like he would Amanda when he found her. He hoped she didn't squeal before he could get to her. The other thing his sister hadn't learned under his tutelage was that you couldn't escape the Wasp.

Chapter Nine

Camilla drove south on the interstate. Rain splattered on the windshield. Her sisters thought she was busy at the candy store, which was how she wanted it. They didn't need to know what kind of errand she was on, especially Tunie. It was one of the reasons she always drove out of town to do it. Her younger sister couldn't handle it. She was already so fragile. Knowing what Camilla did to keep her safe might push Tunie over the edge for the last time. Jubilee was a small town. It wasn't so small that everyone knew each other, but it was small enough that someone as well-known as Camilla would have trouble getting away with clandestine errands.

An eighteen-wheeler sprayed up water, obscuring the windshield so much that she nearly missed the exit. She jerked the car hard to the right, and the back wheels skidded. It didn't go into a spin, thank goodness. The sisters wouldn't be able to pay the deductible for a wreck.

The exit opened onto a two-lane road. It led to a town even smaller than Jubilee, but one where people weren't as likely to know Camilla Bellflower, the candy lady. Water pooled on the edges of the road. Only a few yards past the exit, the pavement was pitted with potholes. Muddy water puddled inside them. Camilla hit one, and the car jarred hard. The argyle sock on the passenger seat fell to the floorboard with a loud jingle. She looked over to make sure nothing had spilled out.

Two miles down the road, she pulled into town. A white-washed cinderblock building with a red garage door sat on the right of the road. A beatdown gas station with only two pumps flanked the left. A rusty green Chevy pickup sat at one of the pumps. A workman caked with gray mud pumped fuel into the green machine.

Camilla remembered a suitor from back in the 1960s who drove a truck like that. It made her feel a bit nostalgic. She missed

Claude Hamner at that moment, which was unusual because most of the time she'd spit on the ground when she thought about him. He'd been her last suitor. Camilla could have been set for life with him. He'd inherited a large farm outside of Jubilee. It came with cattle. Claude wouldn't let her sisters move with her, though. Lily had been a widow for a few years at that point. Tunie had been too immature for a serious relationship. She had tried that and failed miserably. Her sisters needed Camilla, and she needed them. Claude would have nothing to do with it. He'd said if they married, her sisters would be part of her past. To Camilla then as much as now, her sisters were her past, present, future and beyond. They were all part of her essence. Having tragically lost their brother, they now only had each other. She would do anything to keep them together, but Claude didn't understand. She put him aside. Now it seemed only death would separate her and her sisters.

As she drove down the street, Camilla thought about Claude and how that man could kiss. Her toes still tingled at the memory. When he'd died an old bachelor, she'd hoped that he might leave her some money in his will. All she got was turned away from his funeral. His will had stated that he didn't want her there. Some Yankee nephew got everything. Her mind exited memory lane.

A sign with flashing lights shaped like an arrow focused her attention. The black plastic letters on the lit board read: *Mack's Pawn and Title. We buy silver and gold. We sell guns.* There was no question that she'd come to the right place. She pulled into the gravel parking lot. The only other vehicle there was a Ford F150 pickup truck. It was brand new, candy apple red, and glistening in the rain.

Camilla reached down to the passenger-side floorboard and picked up the sock. It was heavy. She regretted that her life had fallen to this level. In the back of her mind, she blamed Claude Hamner and resisted the urge to spit on the floor mat. If he hadn't been so stubborn, things would have been a million times better. She took the short-handled umbrella from the door pocket. Once the door was opened, the black umbrella popped out. She climbed from the car, gripping the sock and the strap of her purse in the same hand. There was no need to lock the doors. Nothing moved on the road. The only person she saw was the muddy workman with the old truck. He had no interest in her Oldsmobile.

The air in the pawn shop smelled musty and full of dust. Metal shelves loaded with all manner of things formed five aisles that led to a long glass counter at the back. The man behind that counter stood up as she walked in. The stub of a lit cigar hung from his mouth. Now the sweet aroma of tobacco smoke wafted to her. For a moment, Camilla again had a memory of Claude. He fancied cheap cigars. It was the reason he eventually died. Emphysema doesn't care how rich you are. Maybe he never married because no one could stand his nasty habit. The need to spit came back. Even in a wretched country pawn shop, she was too much of a lady to hock up something on the floor.

"Can I help you?" the pawn broker asked, not taking the cigar from his mouth.

"Your sign says you buy silver. Is that true?"

He smiled and pulled the chewed stub free of his jowl, placing it in a clear, glass ash tray. "That would be right. I also sell guns. Can't trade silver for a gun though."

"I'm not interested in a gun," Camilla said, stopping at the counter.

She sat her purse and the sock on the glass top. The sock made the heavy metallic jangle again. The pawn broker smiled. He knew the sound. She'd seen that look in many a broker's eye when she'd brought in other socks or old Crown Royal bags.

"How much do you have?" he asked.

Camilla opened the sock and poured the contents on the counter. Several small bars of silver glittered in the light followed by marked rounds. She figured they'd fetch about $500. The pawn broker nodded.

"That's a lot of silver. Are you a collector?" he asked.

"My sister is. How much will you give me? Don't try to jerk me around because I'm an old lady. I know the spot."

His countenance changed from shrewd to cautious. He

counted the pieces of silver. Camilla counted with him. She knew how much was in that sock, but her memory needed refreshing. A pawn broker would take advantage of her, or at least try.

"Thirty ounces of silver," he said. "You turn Christ over to the Jews or something?"

"I'm not in much of a joking mood, Mr. Mack," she said. "I reckon that should be worth around $550."

"Pretty close — and I'm not Mack. I bought the place from him and never changed the name. Taxes."

"So how close am I?"

"$500."

Camilla grouped the pieces of silver into a pile and started dropping them back into the sock. The price was not right, no matter how much she missed Bob Barker.

"$510," the pawn broker upped the ante.

She stopped collecting the silver pieces. He was right where she wanted him. In the old days, men stayed wrapped around her little finger. That finger might be wrinkled and a little gnarled, but she could still twist them.

"$525. No other offers. I'll walk. There's a dozen places that will buy silver between here and Jubilee."

"You drive a hard bargain."

"I have to. The business world isn't for sweet little old ladies."

The pawn broker nodded. They shook on the price. He gave her the cash and a receipt. She took the money, shoved it in her purse, and headed back to Jubilee. That $525 would keep the house in their names for another few weeks. Her sisters had no idea how little money her shop actually made. If it wasn't for her stash of treasures, they'd have lost their home a long time ago. She couldn't stand the idea of the sisters being out on the street or even worse, separated. The Bellflower sisters were never meant to be separated. All of her life had been focused on maintaining the family unit. Fate had seen to it by leaving her unmarried, Lily widowed so young, and Tunie's mind softened to the point she couldn't always remember what she'd done.

Chapter Ten

Vince drove down Dickerson Pike. He'd spent the night in a dive motel out near the interstate. Sleep hadn't come easy because of a vicious storm that blew in. He watched from the window as transformers exploded. The motel had been plunged into darkness, but the place was so cheap none of the management attempted to evacuate the renters as the storm raged. Vince stood in the window and watched. Worry for his safety never bothered him. The fascination with the raw power of the storm overpowered any trepidation he had. Now that it was daylight, Vince realized he felt a little of the fear he should have felt when the storm was going on. Several oak limbs lay on the ground. The windows of the shops across the road were broken. Part of the motel's sign lay in the parking lot, brought down by the strong winds. Now he could see how stupid it had been to not protect himself. If the storm had been stronger, he'd been gone. And then what would happen to his daughter?

The pike didn't have street-side parking, so Vince turned down one of the side streets until he found a convenient place to park. The neighborhood had seen better days. He worried that someone might even break into his car no better than it was. As he exited and headed back toward the Salvation Army shelter, this passed from his mind as did putting money in the meter. He'd blow off a ticket if a meter reader caught him. If a dumb criminal stole his POS car, the crook got what he deserved. He'd be stuck if that happened. The search for Sara Beth would end there. If he found her, they could lay a foundation in Nashville and start a new life.

He walked back down Dickerson Pike. The sun moved toward its noontime peak. The shadows from the buildings had almost evaporated. The smell of the big city filled up his nostrils. The perfume of human stink and diesel fumes always made him nostalgic for home. He'd spent too much time combing the back roads and Podunks of America. His daughter was like some kind of butterfly flitting from here to there, always calling from some far out place like Jubilee, Alabama, or Little Creek, Kansas. He'd not felt the California sun in so long that he almost forgot what it was like. Nashville felt humid and hot. If a May morning could feel that way, he couldn't imagine August.

A few cars sat in the shelter's parking lot, but no one stirred around.

Vince walked into the building. A small desk sat near the door. A harsh looking woman with a name tag introducing her as Dale sat behind it. The telephone rang as he stepped up to the desk. She snatched up the receiver and held up a finger, motioning for him to wait a minute.

"Salvation Army," she said, and listened. "We are a rescue shelter. It's first come, first served. We open to the public around 3:30 in the afternoon. Have a good day."

As soon as the receiver was back on the cradle, Dale looked at Vince. He saw the cynicism in her eyes. She had worked at her job far too long. It had zapped away all of her Southern hospitality.

"I need some help," Vince said.

"The shelter's closed right now. Come back at 3:30 this afternoon."

"I don't need a bed. I'm looking for my daughter. The last I heard she was heading to Nashville. I've got no idea where she is, so I thought I'd start here," Vince said.

"Lots of girls head here. They try to make it in the music business and don't," Dale said.

"That's not why she came. We had a specific trip here a few years ago. It holds a special place in my heart. I believe it does in hers too. I've been trying to catch up with her for over a year," Vince said. "I'm so close. Can you do anything to help me?"

"Hold on." Dale picked up the phone. She called someone and whispered into the receiver. She looked back at him. "One of our social workers will be out here in a moment."

Vince nodded and looked around. The place looked like most of the other shelters he'd visited to ask about Sara Beth. This one smelled a little better. After a few minutes, a young woman, probably right out of college, walked into the lobby. She dressed to look twenty years older. The purple pants suit hung off her. She tried to hide her youthful figure under the too large garment. Her shoes were square-toed and matronly. She put her hand out to him. He took it. The feel of such a young hand in his sent a small shudder through his body. He hoped she hadn't noticed. It had been too long since he'd touched such a pretty woman.

"I'm Tiffany," she said. "Dale told me you are looking for your daughter."

"That's right. I got word that she might be in Nashville, so I decided to start looking here. I've had some success doing that in other cities. Plus, I told her to always go to the Salvation Army first."

"Have you been looking for her for a while?" Tiffany asked.

"At least a year," Vince said. "She stays one step ahead of me."

"Come back to my office. I've got the log book for the last few nights, and we'll see if we can find her."

He followed her down a hallway that was lined with open office doors. Various people did various things in the offices. It looked like any other office suite he'd ever been in. Tiffany's office was at the end beside the restrooms. He figured that was the worst office in the place and reserved for the newest employees. She walked in and sat behind her desk. He sat in an orange vinyl chair across from her.

"What's her name?" Tiffany asked.

"Sara Elizabeth Green, but she might be listed as Beth Green."

Tiffany ran her finger down the names on the roster. She turned to another page. This went on for about three minutes. Finally, Tiffany looked up at him.

"I'm sorry I don't see anyone named Sara Elizabeth or Beth Green. I don't see any Sara Beths or Beths at all. There are a few Greens."

"She used the name Persephone Song at a bed and breakfast down in Alabama," Vince said.

Tiffany shook her head. "No one by that name has been here. It would have stuck in my mind. The three Greens in the book are Marcus Green, Tameka Green and Juanita Green."

"I suppose she's not made it here," Vince said.

"There are lots of other shelters in Nashville. Maybe she's at one of those." Tiffany took out a piece of paper with different emergency shelters listed on it and handed it to him.

"Thank you. Can I use one of the phones here to do that? I'm out of minutes on mine."

"Follow me."

He followed the young social worker to an empty office that was being used as a supply room. A telephone sat on the floor. She showed him how to get an outside line. He started calling around. After nearly an hour and a dozen shelters, Vince gave up and left the Salvation Army.

When he got to his car, he saw a yellow slip of paper clamped beneath his windshield wiper. True to form, the city had ticketed him for not feeding the meter. Vince slid the paper out and tossed it to the ground. For some reason, tossing the ticket made him feel like Sara Beth had never come to Nashville and had never intended to.

Despite the futility of it, Vince called a few other shelters with his remaining cell phone minutes. After all those calls came back cold, he decided to head south to Miami where Woodchuck had gone. Sara Beth might have changed her mind once she got to Tennessee, or she might have gotten tired of waiting for her father to show up.

The last he'd heard from Mary, Elizabeth's mother, she'd lived around the Miami area. With luck, he might find his daughter with her.

But he knew thirteen years was a long time to hang around a place, especially for Mary. If she'd kept up the lifestyle that had lured her away from her family, Mary was probably dead, rotting away in the heat of some potter's field out on an island. Or she might have been long digested in some alligator's stomach after ticking off the wrong drug dealer. It didn't matter though, Miami was the only logical place to go next. Vince would have to roll the dice and try his luck.

***

Lily walked into Bellflower's Candies and Sweets. The soothing aroma of cooking sugar filled the place, but Camilla was not there. No one was in the shop. The lack of customers didn't surprise her. It was early afternoon. The lunch rush would have been over, and the after-schoolers hadn't arrived yet. Camilla came from the back, wiping her hands on her apron.

"What are you doing here?" Camilla asked.

"I can't come by our store?" Lily asked.

"It's my store," Camilla corrected. "You and Tunie took the house. I took the shop. If you want to come here every day and slave over a hot stove working with boiling sugar, then we can talk."

"I don't want that," Lily said. "You don't either. My record of making candy is probably worse than Tunie's."

"I know. So, why are you here?"

"I found something while I was cleaning our bathroom," Lily said.

She took a step behind the counter, but Camilla blocked her. Her sister seemed to be acting a little strange. Earlier in the day when Lily had dropped by to show her what she'd found, Camilla wasn't there, and the shop was closed up tight. It looked like she'd not even opened it yet.

"What is it?" Camilla asked.

"This."

Lily took a necklace from her pocket and put it on the counter. The ruby pendant shimmered in the light. The chain curled underneath it. It was a pillow cut and pretty. She couldn't believe her eyes when she found it.

"Where did you find that?" Camilla snatched if off the counter and held up to the light to look through the stone.

"In our bathroom behind the sink," Lily said. "It's the necklace that girl, Persephone, had. Remember, we talked about how pretty it was?"

43

"I remember. It's a wonder how a girl like that didn't pawn it for drug money or get her throat slit for it," Camilla said. "That stone must be at least a carat."

"I brought it here to put in the store's safe. I don't like the idea of keeping it at the house. We took on some guests," Lily said. "That's why I was giving our bathroom such a good scrub."

Camilla curled the chain and ruby into her hand and dug in a cabinet behind her. She brought out a Ziploc baggie and put the necklace it. She ran her finger on the seal to close it tight. "That's a good idea. I'll put it in the safe when I go back to check on my pralines. I've got a batch cooling right now. I was mixing in the pecans when you came in."

Lily nodded, happy to hear that Camilla had been working in the kitchen. Sometimes she wondered if her sister did anything at the store. Camilla didn't realize that Lily knew how little money the shop made. But somehow her sister always found a way to pay the bills. Lily hoped Camilla wasn't doing something illegal. Camilla liked the program *Breaking Bad*, and a candy shop would be the perfect cover for making methamphetamine.

"I came by earlier to drop that off, and the place was closed," Lily said.

Camilla gave her a suspicious look. "I had errands to run this morning."

"I don't remember you telling us about errands," Lily said.

"I have errands that don't involve you two. I didn't realize that I needed to let my sisters know every move I make, like I was on parole or something."

"You don't. It seemed strange."

"It's not. I do it all the time." Camilla put the Ziploc bag containing the necklace in her apron pocket. "I made a mortgage payment for this month while I was out. We keep the house for a bit longer."

"What about the power bill? It's overdue at least two months."

Camilla narrowed her eyes. "I can only pay one thing at a time. I have to keep this place paid up as well. You said we've got guests. Are they paying guests, or more bums you and Tunie felt sorry for?"

Lily felt her ire rising. Camilla, for all her love, treated Tunie and her like they were idiots. Lily could see it with Tunie, sometimes, but not with herself. She kept her anger under control. They were both under a lot of stress. Tunie was the only one who slept well at night, not worrying about the money. Their baby sister lived with enough of her own issues.

"They are paying customers, a doctor and his wife. They came down from Saginaw, Michigan, to visit with some cousins. They didn't want to stay at the Roadway Inn, so they found us."

"It's about time. Get the money and pay the power bill with that," Camilla said. "I need to go check on those pralines. School will be out soon, and the little grubbers will be in here for their daily sugar fix."

Lily nodded and left without saying another word. She doubted if any children ever walked into the shop. Things had changed a lot since they were young. The kids of today liked candy bars. They didn't want some old lady's hard candies and weird things like pralines. The only thing she knew that Camilla definitely sold to children were her candied apples and a few suckers. The fair would be there soon enough. Then they would have bill money for at least a few months until the Fall Fling rolled into town.

Chapter Eleven

The Wasp shook the bottle of peppermint schnapps at both of the bums. Each one looked like a dog following a wienie in his master's hand. The urge to kill almost overtook him, but it would be stupid to cut up someone. There were other ways to satisfy the itch.

The evening news had reported that the Arkansas State Police found what they believed to be the body of the notorious serial killer, the Peppermint Slasher.

He hated that nickname and had thought of writing a letter to the *Los Angeles Times* declaring himself as the Wasp. Enough true crime books and forensic TV shows had told him the easiest way to get caught was to start writing letters. He knew he wasn't as clever as his idols, the Zodiac Killer or Jack the Ripper, men who killed and taunted and never got caught. A mysterious pair forever written in history with blood.

"How much do you want this?" The Wasp held out a bottle of booze.

"Don't tease me," said the bum that looked like a young Ernest Borgnine with a fluffy beard.

"I'm not teasing," the Wasp said. "I want to know which one of you wants it more."

"I do," answered the other bum who looked like a fat, unkempt version of Danny Trejo.

"Give it to me, man," Ernest Borgnine said. "I'll do things for you. Things like you ain't never felt."

"Faggot," Danny Trejo said. "I can get you stuff, man."

"Fight each other," the Wasp said. "The winner takes all."

As soon as he said the words, Ernest Borgnine sucker-punched the other bum. The two men began to bare-knuckle box in the narrow alleyway the Wasp had staked out earlier as a perfect venue for the event. A deep sensation of pleasure welled up inside him. The Danny Trejo bum held the advantage. His blows hit the other bum with the sound of a cracking whip. Ernest Borgnine hit the ground. The other kicked him in the stomach.

The Wasp's pleasure began to wane. The fight was ending too soon. The itch came back. He licked his lips as he thought of a way to prolong the experience. His knife rested in the scabbard at the small of his back. Two birds could be handled with one stone. He slipped his free hand behind him and pulled out the large skinning knife. With it hidden behind his back, he stepped up to the brawlers.

"Break clean," he said like a real boxing referee. "Give the man a chance to stand up. I can't stand to see something so one-sided."

"I was winning," the Danny Trejo bum said. He reached for the bottle of schnapps.

The Wasp snatched it away and clucked his tongue. "I'll smash it. This fight is to the death."

"I was about to get to that," Trejo said.

"I was a long way from dying," Borgnine said.

The Wasp looked at him. "Prove it."

He shoved the knife at Borgnine and stepped back. A look of glee crossed the bum's face. The Wasp knew the drunk could almost taste the minty freshness of the schnapps, reveling in the way it would burn going down. The Wasp liked the look of hope on Borgnine's face, but the look of terror on Trejo's face was what brought back the feeling of supreme pleasure.

The Trejo bum moved away from the other one. He stumbled over some debris strewn in the alleyway. The bum with the knife lunged. The blade cut into Trejo's leg. It went deep and came free glistening with dark blood. The sight of the red stuff sent the Wasp's heart fluttering. He dug into his pocket and brought out a peppermint disc. The taste of it washed over his tongue. Nothing was better than the first taste of peppermint while watching death. The only joy he remembered as a child was peppermint. An old woman who lived beside him would give him the candy when his grandmother would beat him and put him out of the house without dinner. To the Wasp, peppermint equaled love.

The excitement built. The injured bum grabbed the lid of a metal trashcan and slammed it against the knife-wielding one. The bloody knife came free. It clattered across the pavement. Trejo pushed Borgnine down with the trash lid and snatched up the knife. As Borgnine rallied, the other bum plunged the knife into his gut. The heavily bearded bum bent over and then fell to the ground. Trejo leapt on him and stabbed him multiple times in the gut. A gut stab sounded like nothing else. It played the oboe in a symphony of murder. Trejo was caught up in the blood lust. The Wasp chuckled to himself. He knew the feeling and relished it.

"Don't waste all your energy on the gut. Put some in the chest," the Wasp said. "Feel the difference."

Trejo started stabbing Borgnine in the chest. "I can feel it."

The Wasp heard the change in the music of murder. Now the viola joined the song.

"Cut up his face. It's like carving an exquisite jack-o'-lantern."

The bum did that. Once the blood started to pool at the Wasp's feet, he told the bum to stop. Trejo obeyed. Per their deal, the Wasp gave him the bottle. The bum tore off the cap and downed a large slug of the stuff without realizing the cap had been previously removed and replaced.

The Wasp watched with renewed glee as the winner finished the bottle. The heavy peppermint flavoring in the booze hid the taste of poison. When the bottle was empty, the Trejo bum tossed it at the dead one. The glass shattered on the pavement.

"Was it worth it?" the Wasp asked.

"Yeah, I was getting the shakes."

"Looks like you still have them."

The Danny Trejo bum's hands quaked. Then his legs did the same. His face contorted, and his neck pulled his head to his shoulder. Froth broke from his lips. His tongue lolled out. Then he hit the pavement with a few hard convulsions like those of a grand mal seizure.

The Wasp liked the results of what he'd dissolved in the schnapps. It played as a subtle crescendo to his opus of slaughter.

The bum bit into his tongue. Blood spurted into the air and

mixed with the froth bubbling from his mouth. His teeth sank deeper. A spasm tossed him to his side, and his tongue fell free to the ground. The Wasp giggled like a child watching a Looney Tunes cartoon. This was better than giving a meth whore a Glasgow grin. He filed the idea of poisoning in the back of his mind. It wasn't the first time he'd gotten homeless men to fight to the death, but it was the first time he'd ever poisoned the winner. He liked it. He liked it a lot. It was almost as satisfying as killing with his own hands, and a whole lot cleaner.

The experience would hold him over until he could kill again. Tomorrow he planned to put Memphis behind him. He'd searched all day at the best spots to locate people on the run. His *sister* wasn't there. She wasn't much for the Blues anyway. Salsa was more her thing.

The convulsing bum gave his last spasmodic jerk. Satisfied that Danny Trejo's homeless twin was dead, the Wasp walked out of the alley like he was walking out of a good concert. The last of the peppermint candy melted away in his mouth, leaving its sweet aftertaste.

Chapter Twelve

Vince pawned the last thing he had of any value somewhere around Gainesville, Florida. With a half-carat ruby set in a wide gold ban, it matched Sara Beth's sweet 16 pendant. He'd hated to part with it but had to find her.

The ring fetched him more than enough money for gas to Miami and enough to get him elsewhere if needed. He thought about how much he would miss that ring as he entered Miami-Dade County. Rain poured, and thunder rumbled. Cars raced down the interstate. It felt like he drove on some NASCAR racetrack. The 18-wheeler ahead of him sprayed so much water that the windshield wipers couldn't keep up. He nearly missed the exit to a truck stop he'd been watching for.

He parked in front of an attached restaurant. The rain soaked him when he ran for the door. The smell of frying food comforted him. He seated himself and took the laminated menu from behind the napkin dispenser. The pictures on the card made his mouth water. He hadn't eaten a real meal in a while. Despite having a large sum of money burning a hole in his pocket, he'd only eaten canned meats and pickles on the road from Tennessee. The idea of another Vienna sausage nearly made him vomit. The real reason he'd stopped at this particular place was Mary used to work here. It was a long shot that she would have spent the last dozen years waiting tables at the same greasy spoon, but he had to try.

"What can I get you to drink?" the waitress asked.

"Coke, very little ice," Vince said.

"Pepsi, okay?"

"Not really, but if it's what you've got, it's what you've got. I'm ready to order too."

"Go ahead."

"I want one of these jumbo hamburger steaks with grilled onions, mashed potatoes, a large order of fried cheese sticks, and a side salad with Thousand Island dressing on the side."

"Hungry? Must have been on the road a long time."

"For a while. All I've been eating is camping food," he said.

"Your company doesn't pay you well?"

"I'm not a trucker. I'm looking for someone. Two someones actually. Maybe you know one of them. She used to be a waitress here." Vince took a good look at the waitress for the first time. She looked older than her age, much older than he'd expected. Time had not treated his ex-wife well. "Mary?"

She squinted at him and a look of recognition crossed her face. "Vince? What are you doing here?"

"I'm looking for Sara Beth," he said. "She hasn't contacted you, has she?"

"Sara Beth? No, I haven't heard from her in a long time. The last time I heard anything was when she sent me a high school graduation announcement. What's happened?" Mary sat down in the booth across from him.

"She ran off with a guy named Woodchuck. I've been chasing after her for over a year."

"What about your job?" Mary asked.

"Lost it and the house. I had to pawn everything for enough money to get here," he said.

"Is she in Miami?"

"I don't know. I tracked her to this town in Alabama called Jubilee. She left a bed and breakfast there headed to Nashville, but I couldn't find anything about her there, not a single trace."

"It's a big city."

Vince shook his head. "I've been tracking her for a long time. You learn where to go and who to ask. I've been in bigger towns and gotten nibbles fairly quickly. Nothing this time."

"Why Miami?"

"Woodchuck came here. I had hoped she might track you down if you were still around. It's been thirteen years since I heard from you, so it was a roll of the dice."

"I'll get you that food," Mary said. "On me. Then you can stay at my place. We'll start looking for her tomorrow. I've got a lot of friends around here. If she's in town, they'll know it."

Vince hated Mary. She'd screwed him in two ways. One resulted in his daughter, who he loved more than life. The other was when she left them high and dry in California. Despite his distaste for her, he'd take her up on the offer. It was the least she could do, and it might help track down Sara Beth and finally end his trek for good. He needed to reserve his remaining money as well. He ate, and after her shift ended, they left.

Mary lived in a one bedroom apartment in a part of town that looked like a dozen other towns, but not what he expected Miami to be like. It lacked palm trees and pastel-painted buildings. Instead the houses were blocky and white. If the barren yards had trees, they were pines. A dog barked under the window most of the night, but it was better than sleeping in his car at a rest stop. The couch he slept on was at least a convertible.

With the sun up, he sat at the small round table near the front window drinking a cup of Sanka. Mary brought over two old dinner plates with scrambled eggs, toast, and what he was sure was grits, although he'd never had them. Butter melted atop the gritty pile of white stuff.

"Sorry about the coffee," she said. "I usually don't drink it. I keep the Sanka for the occasions I might want some."

"No problem."

He started on the breakfast. It wasn't the best he'd ever had, but like his poor night's sleep, it was better than sardines on crackers. Even the grits were good. He had no idea why more people didn't eat them. Mary watched him more than she ate. It made him uncomfortable. He figured she was contemplating how their lives had crashed back together.

"I've taken off a few days," she said. "So I can help you search."

"You didn't have to do that. I've been on her trail for a while. I know how to navigate the landscape looking for her."

"Of course I have to. She's my daughter." Mary ate a corner off her toast. "I might not have ever acted like it, but I have regrets. Ever since I got sober, the guilt has eaten at me so much to find you two, but I had no idea where to start."

"We've been in the same place since you left," Vince said. "Except for the last year. Sara Beth went rebellious in her teens. She didn't have a strong female role model. I worked a lot. Too much. She fell in with the wrong crowd. The next thing I know, she's nineteen, hanging with this redheaded freak show named Woodchuck, and she's gone, baby, gone."

"I'm sorry," Mary said. "I should have been there."

"Yes, you should have, but that's the past. Who do you know that might help us find her?"

"I've got a cop friend. He comes into the truck stop a lot. I texted him last night. He says the first place to try is out near the beach. Apparently, there's some kind of youth hostel out there. He told me that the police end up there a lot because of drugs."

"Do you have the address?"

"Of course."

Vince finished off the Sanka with one swallow. He stood, leaving the remains of his breakfast on the plate.

"Let's go. We need to get there before they have a chance to leave," he said.

"It's still early."

"They'll be out early to start panhandling." He looked at her and could tell she was not convinced. "I keep telling you that I've been doing this for a while. I know the pattern. They need money for food and drugs. Neither one of those come for free. You ought to know that."

Mary nodded and finished her coffee. "Yeah, I know that firsthand. One of the lessons I wish I could have learned a lot easier—or not at all."

They left the apartment and drove his car across the city. Mary navigated. They found the place a few blocks from the beach. The neighborhood looked like what he'd imagined Miami to be, palm trees everywhere and pastel paint jobs, the postcard picture of Miami.

The hostel appeared to be an old hotel that had seen its better days before Castro took over Cuba. A group of women whose clothes told him they were young, but whose faces looked far too old, stepped out into the sunshine. Vince hurried to them before they could get away. The women appeared leery of him, at first ignoring his polite calls of *excuse me.* They stopped when he said he would pay them for information.

"What can we help you with?" the one with the stringy red hair asked.

"We're looking for someone." Vince pointed to Mary as she joined him.

"Isn't everyone?" a brunette said.

"It's our daughter," Mary said. "Her name is Sara Elizabeth Green." She held out the photograph of her daughter that Vince had.

"Lots of girls look like that," a dirty blonde answered.

Vince took out a $20 and handed it to the redhead. "She might be calling herself Persephone. She's been traveling with a guy who calls himself Woodchuck."

"Ugly redheaded guy?" the brunette asked.

"That's him," Vince said.

"He's staying here, but he's alone," the redhead said. "Came alone as far as I know."

"He didn't come alone last night, did he, Fifi?" the blonde said to the redhead.

"Is he here right now?" Mary asked.

"I guess," the blonde said.

Vince gave her a disdainful look. "That's fine. We can go in and check. I'm tapped out."

The women looked disappointed, but they had told him enough. He took Mary by the arm and led her into the hostel. The lobby looked swanky compared to the rundown façade. The furniture was dated but kept in a pristine condition. The whole place felt like a Roaring Twenties revival. Potted palms flanked a staircase. An art deco check-in counter sat against a far wall. A pigeon-hole cabinet housed the room keys. A woman with blue and pink striped hair sat behind the counter. Vince walked up to her, and she gave him a strange look.

"You are a bit old for a hostel, no?" she asked with a heavy Russian accent.

"I'm not here for a room," he said.

"Are you a cop?"

"Far from it," Mary said.

"We're looking for someone," Vince said. "My daughter, to be exact."

"Lots of daughters come here," the register woman said. "You'll have to be more specific."

"Sara Elizabeth Green. She would have come in with a guy calling himself Woodchuck. I've got no idea what his real name is," Vince said.

"Sara Beth?" a voice said from behind them.

Vince turned around to the see a gangly red-haired boy with a greasy ponytail. It was Woodchuck, skinnier and uglier than he'd remembered.

"Woodchuck," Vince said.

"This is Woodchuck? You have found him," the register woman said. "Another satisfied customer."

"Where is she?" Vince asked.

"I don't know," Woodchuck said. "Who are you?"

"I'm her dad, and this is her mother," Vince said.

"Mr. Green," he put his hand out. "Great to meet you. She talked about you all the time. I'm sorry we never got to meet back in California."

Vince did not give him his hand. "You'll excuse me if I'm less than pleased to see you, Woodchuck. Where is my daughter?"

"I don't know. The last time I saw her was in Alabama at some bed-and-breakfast flop house run by three grannies. They said she'd headed off to Nashville or Knoxville, someplace in Tennessee. Me and the guys I was with kept on our way here. I haven't heard from her since. I figured she got tired and went home," he said.

"She didn't," Mary said, "and I don't believe you. I've known a lot dudes like you. None of you tell a straight story."

"I believe him," Vince said. "I met the same three old ladies.

They told me the same thing. It's why I went to Nashville."

"She didn't go home?" Woodchuck asked.

"I don't know. I haven't heard from her. The last place she called me from was in Alabama. I went looking for her there and then went to Nashville. I didn't find her in either place."

"Dude," Woodchuck said. "Do you think she's safe? I'd hate to know something happened to her. I dug her."

"I don't know," Vince said.

He looked at Mary. She typed into her phone and then looked back at him. The phone beeped. She stared at it.

"I texted Sara Beth's description and her picture to my police friend. He's going to do a missing person's report," she said. "He says it might help, but it's a long shot."

"Why?" Vince asked.

"Apparently, a serial killer was found dead after a car accident around Memphis," Mary answered with a worried look. "He'd been killing young women who were hitchhiking. Not all the victims have been identified yet."

"She supposedly went to Nashville," Vince said. "They aren't that close together."

"My friend still wanted us to know. He also wondered if we want Woodchuck here arrested," Mary said.

"For what?" Woodchuck asked.

"Yeah, for what?" Vince agreed. "They can't arrest someone for being a jackass."

"That's not very nice," Woodchuck said. "You don't even know me."

"I know you stole my daughter away, and haven't seen fit to look for her or try to contact me," Vince said. "Calling you a jackass was a compliment."

Woodchuck puffed up and walked away. Vince took this as a victory and sat on a sofa. The end of the road had finally come, and it depressed him more than he had ever imagined. Mary sat by him and put her hand on his knee. He knocked it off.

Chapter Thirteen

The Wasp stood on the bank of the Mississippi River. The water moved past him in the night, dark and quiet. The road he'd used to get to the spot was one engineers used when they worked on the levees. No one would be venturing down here until the morning and maybe not for days. The sound of a barge rolling down the Big Muddy stirred something inside him. It felt like nostalgia. He had no idea why it would stir that kind of emotion in him. The Mississippi River meant little to him beyond memories of tenth grade English, when he read *The Adventures of Huckleberry Finn*. At that moment, he felt a little bit like Huck, both of them rascals in transition to new circumstances. He supposed they both needed a little civilizing as well.

The family of Jeff Henderson reported him missing. Those clever policemen pulled the records and determined that the charred remains believed to be the infamous Peppermint Slasher were in fact another murder victim.

The barge churned past. He watched its lights fade as it disappeared around a bend in the river. Once the sound of the wake splashing against the shore stopped, the Wasp opened the trunk of the Caprice Classic he'd won from a wannabe pimp in a game of back-alley craps. The dim glow of the trunk light illuminated a body wrapped in a motel duvet cover. The Wasp studied it. The body of a beautiful young woman lay beneath the cheap mottled bedspread. She might be the prettiest girl he'd ever killed. In many ways, she reminded him of his wayward *sister*. His little prodigal student evaded him thus far, but this victim was so much like her that it gave him a cathartic release.

She felt a lot heavier than when he'd put her in the trunk. At that time, he was still full of the adrenalin from the kill. It always gave him a boost of strength. He carried her to the edge of the levee that rose several feet above the river banks. When he sat her on the edge, he uncovered her face. Only a slip of moon shone in the sky. It gave enough blue light to see her lovely face, calm and ashen, one last time. With her eyes closed, he could have mistaken her for sleeping, if not for the gaping smile he'd cut in her neck. The poor girl didn't even know she was being murdered until he ran his knife across her lovely throat.

The girl with purple hair and rosy cheeks had sold herself for a little money. She didn't look like an addict even when she was naked. She was still tight, so he knew that she'd not been a prostitute for long. Her story: She was down on her luck after having run away with a guy. Memphis is as far as she'd made it before her luck ran out.

She did a lot of things for the few dollars he flashed at her. They'd taken a shower afterwards. He made sure he carefully bathed her to scrub off any stray DNA. He cut her throat in the bathtub while fingering her rectum, so he could shove the peppermint disc inside. Poor girl never expected it. That made him sad. All of his victims deserved to know that they were being killed by a famous serial killer.

The Wasp took one last look, ached a little for her beauty, and then kicked her off the levee to roll down the embankment and into the river. Unfortunately, they weren't in Louisiana so there wouldn't be any alligators to drag off her body. The police would find her, know that he had been there, and that was okay. They'd never expect him to be driving some pimp's Chevy, painted iridescent green and sporting fancy chrome rims. The windows were tinted so darkly no one could see him.

The girl's body hit the water with a splash. The Wasp got into the car and left. His destination was somewhere to the southeast. He could put several hundred miles on the car until he had to abandon it. By dawn, he'd be somewhere deep in Mississippi. The cops would expect him to follow the interstate. He took the road less traveled, so the screws would be taking a wild goose chase when they chose the other route. Once enough time or distance had passed, he'd return to following the interstate.

Chapter Fourteen

Camilla walked into the mayor's office. His assistant, Sandra Bartlett, looked up from her computer screen when she heard Camilla's hard-soled shoes clomping on the floor. She smiled.

"I brought you something," Camilla said.

"I hope it's a treat," Sandra said.

"It's this," Camilla reached into her tote bag and pulled out a manila envelope. "My paperwork to get a booth at the fair."

Sandra looked disappointed as she took the envelope. "I sure was hoping for something sweeter?"

"Come down to the fair and get a candy apple," Camilla said. "Business hasn't been too good lately. I can't go around giving away goodies to everyone I encounter."

"I'm sorry. You're right. You can't do that."

Camilla smiled at her and reached back into her tote bag. She took out a praline wrapped in cellophane. Sandra's eyes widened when she saw it. Anytime Camilla brought out some kind of goody, whoever was on the receiving end looked like a kid on Christmas. She knew she was a good candy maker, but if people liked her stuff as well as they appeared to when she gave them gifts, they sure didn't show it by actually buying from her store.

"Thank you," Sandra said.

The secretary took the form from the envelope. She stamped it *approved* without looking at it or at the check attached with a paper clip. Camilla liked the idea that she could stiff them and no one would be the wiser. Some melted sugar and pecans could do amazing things.

"Am I going to be in the same place as usual?" she asked.

"Of course," Sandra said with a mouthful of praline. "On the midway, close to the merry-go-round. The mayor will see to it."

"Good."

Camilla smiled and turned to leave. Luckily, the mayor was also the chair of the fair committee and had wonderful sway over the carnies. If it were up to those traveling gypsies, they'd have her stationed in the back where the livestock exhibits were kept. Nothing made people's mouth water more than the smell of caramel apples and manure. As she walked out the door, she heard the mayor's voice boom from his office.

"Is that Camilla Bellflower?" he asked.

"She's just leaving," Sandra answered.

"Call her back."

"Camilla, wait. The mayor wants you."

Camilla stopped on the other side of the door. Jeremiah Maxwell would be wanting his bribe as well. She turned around and walked back into the office. The mayor stood in the doorway to the alcove where he conducted his business.

"You didn't forget me, did you?" he asked, smiling his politician's smile.

"'Course not," Camilla said. "Here."

She tossed him a praline wrapped in cellophane. He caught it and shook his head at the prize. A sound of delicious satisfaction came from his lips. Camilla turned to leave again.

"Hold up a minute," he said. "Come in here. I need to talk to you."

"Can't we do it out here?" she asked.

"I need to talk with you in private. I think you'd want it that way."

Jeremiah stepped back into his office. Camilla followed. He closed the door behind her. She'd never been to his executive suite. The window behind his heavy wooden desk looked out on the town square. The Confederate monument stood in the middle of the small green space. A flag flapped in the wind. The mayor sat behind his desk and offered her one of his visitor seats. She sank into the plush green velour of the cushion.

"Camilla, I've been getting complaints about a strange smell coming from behind your shop," he said.

"Smell? What kind of smell?" Her mouth felt parched

"A bad one. Folks says it smells like something dead is back there."

"I've not smelled anything," Camilla said. This was true. She hadn't smelled anything out of the ordinary, all things considered.

"They say it's been like that for a while now."

"Maybe a coon or possum died back there," Camilla said.

"Those would quit stinking after a couple of days. This has been too long for that." Jeremiah turned his chair and looked out the window. "You can't think of anything else?"

She thought for a moment, looking for the answer. "I have a grease trap out there that I keep my used grease from the fryers in. When it gets warm it can smell something fierce, but usually if the lid is down, it's not noticeable."

He turned back around. "I've smelled one of those things behind Jack's before. I almost vomited on the spot. You have one of those?"

"I occasionally make savory food, too," she said. "And some other fried treats from time to time. If you'd come by and buy something instead of waiting on bribes for my prime fair real estate, you might know that."

A guilty looked crossed Jeremiah's face. He slid the free pralines under some papers as if she didn't know he had it. "You're right. I should visit you more often. I don't know if that is what people are smelling. Those containers stink, but folks are saying this is a rotten smell."

"Maybe a coon or a possum drowned in the stuff. I bet they'd take longer to decompose in there. Could even been more than one. It wouldn't be the first time I've had critters trying to get in the thing."

"Aren't the lids heavy?"

"Yeah, I can't always get them closed properly," Camilla said.

"Do you think there is anything you could do to help with the smell?"

"I can throw some lime back there, until I can get the grease people out to empty the bin. It might help," Camilla said.

"Sounds good. Thanks for your time."

"It's no problem."

Camilla stood and left his office. As she walked back to her car, the idea of how stupid she had been almost overwhelmed her. She'd have to swing past the hardware store on the way back to the shop to pick up some lime. The neighbors didn't need to complain about the smell anymore. The mayor didn't need to poke around, and her sisters, especially Tunie, needed to know nothing about it.

***

Lily brought in a tray with some glasses of tea on it. A little saucer held a few pralines that Camilla had brought home from the shop, claiming they were scorched. They tasted fine to Lily, but Camilla was the candy maker not her. Mr. Blake sat on the sofa in the parlor. He held his briefcase on his lap. Lily set the tray on the coffee table. He took a glass and a confection. She sat in the armchair opposite him.

"I wasn't expecting a visit from you, Mr. Blake," she tried not to sound nervous.

"I hadn't expected to come out here," he said. "This is a really good praline."

"Camilla made them at her shop," Lily said. "She's got a knack with candy."

"That she does. I love those apples she makes for the fair every year. It's the only time my kids will eat apples. She should make those at other times of the year. The money would roll in."

Lily smiled. "She does, and it doesn't."

"Oh," Mr. Blake sounded surprised. "I suppose that I should visit her shop more often."

"Why are you paying me this visit?"

Mr. Blake took a swig of the tea and then replaced it on the tray. He opened his briefcase and brought out a single piece of paper. Lily didn't like the look of it. It was thinner than printer paper, and yellow. She knew that meant serious business.

"You're behind on the mortgage," he said.

"Camilla said she paid it a week or so ago."

"She paid $500. You owe close to $10,000 in back payments."

"Let me see that." Lily snatched the paper away.

Most of the numbers on the document were gobblygook to

her. At the bottom *$10,000* was printed with the word *foreclosure*. Her heart sank. She'd known they were behind on the mortgage, but not this much. They couldn't afford the payment. How could Camilla have let them slip so far into debt?

"How long do we have?" she asked.

"I've talked the main office into giving you until after the fair. I know that you always make a large payment after that," Mr. Blake said.

"Camilla never makes *that* much. Can we pay half of it then?"

Mr. Blake shook his head. His eyes looked sad. She felt his empathy.

"It was everything I could do to kick the can that far down the road."

Lily hung her head. She felt like crying. The house had been in their family since the Civil War. It had been spared from the Yankee torches because it was large enough that they used it as a hospital. Somehow her daddy had kept it through the Depression. Now, she and her sisters were going to lose it because they'd had to mortgage it to pay off some bad investments. If Ernie hadn't died so young, none of this would matter. He had to drink moonshine, couldn't resist it. That bad jug gave him the seizure that ended him. She fought back the tears and held her head up.

"What are we supposed to do if we can't make the payment, Mr. Blake? We're old ladies, already working past our prime."

"I don't know. Advertise your bed and breakfast a bit more and see if that would bring in more revenue."

"Have you looked around? There's nothing left in this town to attract people. We've got a truck stop, a Ruby Tuesday's, and an old railroad depot that meth addicts use as a drug house. That's a tourist attraction, isn't it?"

"I understand you're mad, Lily, but I've done everything short of paying your note myself. You do realize I put my job on the line for you ladies."

The front door opened. Camilla walked in still wearing her work apron. The smell of cooked sugar wafted from her. Lily hadn't realized the time. She looked at her sister. A smile beamed on Camilla's face.

"I thought that was your car parked out there, Mr. Blake. What brings you by here?" she asked.

"We can talk about it later," Lily said.

"Is it that bad?" Camilla asked.

"Yes," Mr. Blake answered. "I was telling your sister that the bank is going to foreclose on this property if you don't pay $10,000 by the end of the fair."

"I've never made that much at the fair," Camilla said. "They can't do that. I've been paying."

"A hundred here and five hundred there hasn't cut it," Mr. Blake said. "I've done everything I can."

"No, quite," Camilla said. She looked at Lily. "Does Tunie know?"

"Not yet."

"Don't tell her. She'll go into hysterics," Camilla said.

"I think I better go," Mr. Blake stood up. He took his briefcase and pushed past Camilla. "By the way, the pralines are fantastic."

"Come by the shop sometime and buy some. You know I need the money."

"I may, especially if you have any apples made up," Mr. Blake said, letting himself out the door.

"Liar," Camilla said and turned to Lily. "So?"

"So what?" Lily answered back. "I've got nothing. The money from the last guests went to the power company today. If we don't make the money at the fair, we're bag ladies."

Camilla snarled and stomped off to her room. Her heavy footfalls sent dust fluttering down from the ceiling. Lily put her face in her hands and cried. They had been together for so long. She couldn't imagine what they would do if they were separated at this point in life. They had become too dependent on each other. Tunie needed them worst of all. If something like that happened to them, she'd end up in the crazy house. No one else had ever helped them nor even had much concern for their well-being. The Bellflower sisters only had each other. For the first time in a long time, Lily felt the fear that Camilla always had. At that moment, everything seemed hopeless, and she was afraid of being alone. It would wither them all if they lost the house. Each would curl up and die, like flowers in oppressive heat.

She lifted her head and wiped at her eyes with the heel of her palms. A small picture of her Ernie hung on the wall. They hadn't been married long, but during that time, he had shown good sense when it came to money. The only thing he hadn't shown good sense about was booze. Ernie always made sure that the bills were paid and that they had food on the table to eat. He even allowed Camilla and Tunie to stay for extended periods.

Although it would have been a giant burden at the time, Lily wished they hadn't lost their baby. At least their son might have been able to help her in old age. She wouldn't be wilting away under debt and the near-paralyzing fear of being thrown off her home soil. The tears stopped flowing. This was not the right time for crying. It did nothing to help.

Chapter Fifteen

Vince and Mary sat in a police station waiting room in downtown Memphis. A body matching their daughter's description had been found floating in the Mississippi River. They had driven all night from Miami after they'd gotten the call from Mary's friend on the force. Somewhere near Dothan, Alabama, he and Mary had switched driving duties. He had gotten some fitful sleep but not much.

It seemed like they'd been sitting there forever. Vince couldn't keep track of how many uniformed officers came in and out of the door. None of them did more than nod their heads. He tapped his feet like a drummer playing the high hat. Mary put her hand on his knee and squeezed. He stopped mostly so she would quit touching him.

"How can you be so calm?" he asked.

"There's nothing we can do by worrying," Mary said. "If it is Sara Beth's body they've found, she's gone. If it's not, we keep looking."

"That seems like a cold way to think about your daughter," Vince said.

"It's how I've learned to cope with life. *Que sera, sera.*"

"Thank you, Doris Day."

A tall officer wearing a blue shirt and gray slacks came from somewhere deep inside the building. He wore his badge on his belt and his pistol in a shoulder holster. He smiled at them. Vince didn't return the sentiment.

"Are you the Greens?" he asked.

"I am," Vince said. "She's not."

The officer's smile wavered but returned. "Are you here about the possible Sara Elizabeth Green, missing person reported from Miami?"

"Yes," Mary answered. "Excuse him. He's been under a lot of stress."

"I understand. I'm detective Stevens. Please come with me."

The officer swept his hand in the direction he'd come. Vince and Mary stood up. They walked a little ahead of Stevens until he took the lead to show them where they were going. Vince didn't care for the detective so far. He seemed interested in humoring them more than anything else.

"I'm sorry to have kept y'all waiting," Stevens said as they stepped into a room with a table and a few chairs. "I was on the phone with the officer who found the body. He was giving me some more details."

They sat down across from each other. The room was cold. Vince crossed his arms to fight off the chill. If it looked like he was displeased, all the better. His little girl might be dead, and this cop kept delaying talking to them. He bubbled with the hot lava of anger. Mary put her hand back on his knee. She gave it another squeeze. He unfolded his arms.

"What do you know?" Mary asked.

"First things first. I need your names." Steven took out a yellow pad and pencil.

"My name is Mary Carruthers. I'm Sara Beth's mother."

He jotted down the name. "Where are you from?"

"Miami, Florida. I'm originally from Oregon. I had Sara Beth while living in California."

Stevens wrote down all the information and looked at Vince. Several seconds passed in silence. Vince wasn't going to answer until he was asked. Detective Stevens wouldn't get off that easy. Vince would make him wait and see how the detective liked being on the other end of that table.

"And you?" the detective asked.

"My name is Vincent Price Green. Yes, I was named after the actor. My mother loved the movie *The Tingler*. I go by Vince. Sara Beth is my daughter. I raised her by myself after her mother took off. I'm from California, but have been wandering the country for over a year chasing after Sara Beth. She ran away with a lovely hippie of a fellow named Woodchuck. I don't know his real name, but he's in Miami so I doubt he was the killer."

"Thank you both." Stevens slid a folder from under his notebook. He tapped it with his long slender finger. "There are pictures of the victim in this folder. I'm going to show them to you so that you can ID the body. If you can't tell anything from the photos, we'll head over to the morgue. If you do identify your daughter, we'll still have to head over to the morgue. Please understand that these pictures are graphic and disturbing."

"Did she suffer?" Mary asked.

Vince didn't want to know the answer. Of everything that mattered, he felt that was the one thing that didn't. If the last moments of his daughter's life had been a torture, he didn't want to know. Being murdered could never be pleasant.

"We can't say how long she would have suffered, but yes, she would have. As best we can tell, she was the victim of a serial killer the FBI is calling the Peppermint Slasher. However, this case is different because the only trademark that says it might have been him was the insertion of a peppermint candy in one of her orifices. It could be a copycat killer."

"Enough," Vince said. The thought of a sadistic killer toying with his daughter and then putting anything into her dead body was almost too much. The idea of some copycat wannabe doing it for attention made things even worse.

Stevens opened the folder and slid the large pictures to them. The photograph on top showed the victim floating face down in the water. Her white naked backside looked like a fish belly. Vince turned to the next picture. This was a close-up of the face from the shoulders up. A jagged gash gaped in her throat. The face was gray from lack of blood and bloated from time in the river. Even with all that, he'd know his daughter if he saw her.

"That's not her," he said.

"Are you sure?" Stevens said.

"Positive." Vince said.

Mary shook her head. "I don't know, it could be."

"You've not seen her in a long time," Vince said. "It's not her."

"It's been a year since you've seen her," Mary replied.

"Some things don't change," Vince said. "She had a scar over her left eye that wouldn't allow an eyebrow to grow there. She got it when she was 16 in a car accident. That girl has both eyebrows."

"It could be artificial," Stevens said.

"How long do you think she was floating there?" Vince asked.

"Around two days," Stevens answered.

"No cosmetic adhesive is going to keep a fake eyebrow on that long. It's not her."

Vince felt relief. Even though he had no idea where to find Sara Beth, he knew she wasn't this victim of a killer with a candy fetish. There was hope that she was still alive.

"I'm happy to hear that it's not your daughter," Stevens said.

"I'm glad, too," Mary said. "You're positive, Vince?"

"I'd swear it on my mother's grave. That is not my daughter."

"I thank you for doing this for me. I can walk you out," Stevens said.

"Can we be alone in here for a minute, please?" Mary said.

"Sure." Stevens got up and left the room.

Vince looked at his daughter's mother. For some reason, he got the feeling that she'd wanted the girl in the river to be Sara Beth so that she could get back to her insignificant life as a truck-stop waitress. At that moment he wanted to smack her as hard as he could.

"I am so happy," she said. "Well, maybe not happy, but relieved."

"So am I," he answered back through his anger.

"What now?"

He thought for a moment. There was only one option. Sara Beth's trail was cold, and there wasn't any way to warm it up but to go back to Jubilee.

"We need to pay another visit to the Bellflower sisters. The ladies who told me, and apparently also told Woodchuck, that Sara Beth had gone to Nashville."

"You don't think they lied, do you?"

"I don't know, but we've got no other leads."

"We could go to Nashville," Mary said.

"That's been done. She wasn't there. Alabama is the only answer."

Something niggled at his mind. The Bellflower sisters hadn't been entirely honest with him. They kept calling Sara Beth *Persephone*. Even if she'd used that name, they'd known it was a fake one like Woodchuck used.

Right then, he wanted to check into a room and sleep for a while. If he stayed awake much longer, he'd go crazy. The stress of identifying the body was more tiring than the long miles he'd traveled.

Chapter Sixteen

Camilla sat straight up in bed, heart pounding so fast her chest felt like it was in a vise. For a moment, she thought she might be having a heart attack. The room around her felt warmer than usual, and the blackness seemed darker than anything she'd ever experienced.

The nightmare still pounded between her temples as reality began to creep into the corners of her mind. The room cooled. The darkness lightened. Her heart rate slowed down. She reached for the glass of water she always kept by her bed. The tepid wetness felt good as it dampened the parched landscape of her mouth. Despite everything around her resetting itself to default, Camilla couldn't shake the feeling of immense loneliness. Her nightmare had been nothing but that, profound waves of loneliness. No images accompanied the feeling. No sounds or echoes filled the dream. Everything had been as black as when she woke, and that loneliness was like something that stalked her in the night and finally enveloped her. She hated that dream.

The floor felt hard on her sore feet as she climbed from her bed. The standing lamp cast a pink light over the room, but the shadows that darkened the corners weren't dispelled. Some light was better than no light. She didn't want to turn on the overhead fixture because it might worry her sisters. They'd come asking why she was up, and what she was up to. There were some things she needed to keep to herself. No good could come from them knowing her plan.

She walked to her closet and opened it. The hinges creaked. Camilla stopped and listened. Nothing moved in the house. She felt silly for thinking her sisters could hear that slight noise. A bomb could explode in the street out front for all Lily and Tunie would know. Those two had hearing problems for a long time. Neither would admit it. Camilla felt blessed to still have most of her hearing. The Lord had seen fit to give her at least that.

Sometimes she wondered why it seemed all he gave her was good hearing.

Once she was satisfied that her sisters still slept, Camilla pulled the string attached to the light in her closet. The naked bulb lit up the small space. She stood on tiptoe and reached as far into the left corner as she could. Her fingers slipped under a stack of quilts and probed until she felt the braided strings of a Crown Royal bag. She pulled the bag free, and it caught on two fingers with a heft that almost made her drop it. The bag would have made quite a racket if it had hit the hardwood floor. Tunie might have come to see if Camilla had fallen out of bed.

Her sister was always concerned about her. This made Camilla sad and happy at the same time. If Tunie only knew how much time and grief her sister had spent making sure that she was always okay and never in trouble. The Silver American Eagle coins in the pouch Camilla held were the perfect example. She'd kept them hidden to keep Tunie from slipping back into a demented state. Any moments of tragedy did that to the poor soul.

Camilla sat down on her bed and put the bag of coins in her lap. They clanked together with the unmistakable sound of pure silver. She knew of no other sound like it. The jingle of the thirty silver coins sounded like hope.

The morning the coins came into her possession had been an unseasonably cold one. Lily was at the grocery store, shopping for the week ahead. Camilla suffered a cold that kept her from opening the shop. She didn't want to expose the children to her germs. Equally during the winter months, she liked to limit her exposure to the pathogens they brought with them into the store. She didn't fight off disease as well as she had in her younger days, a side effect of old age.

Tunie had banged on her bedroom door that cold morning. It rattled the thing on its hinges. Camilla jumped up from bed and hurried across. When she opened it, her baby sister looked as if she might lose her mind. Camilla knew the look to well. She'd seen it many times before.

"What's happened?" she asked.

"It's horrible, Camilla, horrible!" Tunie clutched at her face.

"What is it?"

"Slappy's dead."

Camilla already knew this before her sister said it. As soon as Tunie banged on her door, she knew the bum lay in his bed, cold and stiff. Before she could tell her sister to calm down, Tunie took off down the hall back toward the stairs. Camilla grabbed her robe and tied it around her as she followed her baby sister to the third floor.

The door to the bum's room stood open. Tunie disappeared inside with a long wail when she saw the dead man. Camilla walked in with no drama. The man with his long scruffy beard lay in bed staring straight up at the ceiling with his glazed-over eyes. His mouth hung slack. His right arm dangled off the bed almost touching the floor. A half-eaten piece of red taffy lay under his hand. A paper plate with a dozen more pieces, some white and others red lay on his bedside table.

"What did you do?" Camilla asked her sister.

"Nothing, I just gave him some taffy. He looked so lonely last night. I thought it might cheer him up," Tunie said.

"It cheered him up, all right," Camilla said, stepping up and taking the half-eaten candy from the floor.

She placed it on the plate with the other pieces. The bum, who called himself Slappy, was one of the transients that Tunie had a tendency to pick up, always saying that she felt sorry for them. Camilla felt sorry when she saw them walk into the house. She knew they would never pay their bill because they would never check out.

"You gave him your taffy," Camilla said. "I told you to throw that out. Where have you been hiding it?"

"I don't know what you're talking about," Tunie said.

"How many times do we have to go through this? You killed him, Tunie. You poisoned some taffy and then gave it to him. It's always the red pieces, just like with Ernie all those years ago."

Tunie rubbed her face and pulled at her hair. "I didn't poison him. I didn't make those candies. You did. You make the candies. We need to call the police. We need to get them over here right now."

"They'll carry you off to jail. Do you want to go to prison? They'll call you *Granny*," Camilla said.

"We called the police when Ernie died. He had a heart attack. They said so. Slappy had a heart attack." Tunie continued to pull on her hair.

"Back then, they didn't have the ability to find poisons like they can now. Go get the shovel from the garage and head to the shed out back. Start digging in the far back corner. We've got some room back there," Camilla ordered.

"We need to wait on Lily," Tunie said.

"She doesn't need to know anything about this, or she might start thinking this is what happened to Ernie. Do you want her knowing the truth?"

Tunie blinked hard and twisted her head to the left while still tugging her hair. "No."

"Then get the shovel and start digging. I'll wrap him up in the quilt and start dragging him out there," Camilla said. "We're getting too old for this."

Tunie hurried away, slamming into the doorway as she did. Camilla waited until she heard the back door slam before she took the bum's arm and laid it on his chest. She did the same with the other then took the ends of the quilt and wrapped him inside it. A quick look through the dresser drawers revealed a Crown Royal bag with some silver in it. The coins wouldn't cover his stay but would help. Camilla put the bag into the pocket of her robe and started the process of dragging the vagrant out of the house, hoping to finish before Lily got back.

Despite Mr. Blake's threat, the coins would pay the mortgage and keep the sisters together for at least thirty more days. The bank had always negotiated once money was waved at them. After the silver ran out, only the ruby necklace would remain, and Camilla didn't want to get rid of that yet.

Chapter Seventeen

The Wasp stood behind a rack of small kitchen appliances. He stared through the space between a prototype microwave and a toaster oven that looked like it came off a Russian submarine. An old lady stood at the counter of the pawn shop. She counted out thirty silver American eagles from an argyle sock. He did love a good argyle sock.

"Back again," the pawn broker said with a cigar clenched in his molars.

"What can I say, I need the money," the old lady said.

"Those are American eagles," the pawn broker said. "Where did you pick up that many of them?"

"I purchased them from an exchange," the woman said.

The Wasp watched her intently. He kept as secluded as he could. Something about the lady intrigued him. She'd dressed rather matronly, but the way she held herself belied her grandmotherly appearance. Her stance quivered with the energy of a spring waiting release. Deep inside, she had the soul of a predator. As he looked at the silver glittering on the counter, he wondered where she'd gotten the coins. They had not come to her in an honest way.

"Are you sure?" the pawn broker asked.

"Are you saying I stole them?" She acted like his question infuriated her. The Wasp knew differently. "Are you saying there's not a single thing in this store that isn't hot?"

"I'll give you $525 for them," the pawn broker said.

"You'll give me $540."

"We settled on $525 last time."

"Those were generic bars and rounds. These are American eagles. They'll fetch a bit more because of that—$540."

"Five-hundred thirty, and I don't call the cops on you." The pawn broker took his cigar from his mouth.

The Wasp could tell that the broker was nervous. Something

about the old lady made him that way. He liked her more and more, like he was watching his soul grandmother in action. In reality, his biological grandmother died young from a severe heroin addiction. When he was eight-years-old, he'd found her bloated purple corpse on the toilet with a needle in her arm. The Silver Lady was too classy for drugs, but not too classy for crime. He could tell. She knew how to lie and bluff.

"$535, and I don't call the cops," the old lady said. "I'll throw in some peppermint taffy. My sister messed up the color. People aren't going to buy it like this. They associate red with cherry and white with vanilla." The pawn broker hesitated. "Don't worry. It's not poisoned."

She reached into her large purse and brought out a gallon-size Ziploc bag full of red and white pieces of candy.

"Deal."

They shook hands. The pawn broker counted out the cash on the counter. The Silver Lady folded the bills and slipped them into her purse. As she walked past the rack where the Wasp hid, he opened the door of the microwave and acted like he was examining it. He didn't want her to see his face. Such a clever fox would take note of everything.

She got in her car and pulled from the parking lot. The Wasp stepped out from behind the rack. He approached the section of glass counter that contained hand guns. A snub-nosed .38 lay beside a .45 and .9mm police issue. The pawn broker stepped over to him.

"Can I help you?" he asked.

"How much for the snub nose?" the Wasp asked.

The broker looked him up and down. "I only sell to serious buyers, not bums."

The Wasp smiled and held back the urge to punch the man in his bulbous nose and make his gin blossom bloom. He reached into his pocket and laid a roll of one hundred dollar bills on the counter. "I'm nothing but serious."

"I charge extra for falsified paperwork," the pawn broker said. "I also keep all my *no waiting period* pieces in a separate area."

"I guess we're on the same page because I pay extra for fatsoes to keep their mouths closed," the Wasp said.

The pawn broker smiled and opened a drawer behind him that looked like a panel on the wall. He took out a snub-nosed .38 and placed it on the counter. The Wasp picked it up. The weight felt good. It would be easy to conceal in a pocket. He didn't like using a gun. It took a lot of the fun out of the kill, but he needed to put the cops off his trail. The need to murder was so strong at the moment that he felt like a junkie coming off the horse.

"Got a place to try out this thing?" the Wasp asked.

The pawn broker pointed to a side door with his head. The Wasp looked through the glass. A large round bale of hay spray-painted with a red target sat about three hundred feet behind the building. It backed up to an embankment cordoned off by a high privacy fence.

"Bullets?"

The pawn broker pulled a cardboard box from the glass case. The Wasp dug out five bullets so the broker could see him, but secluded a sixth using an old sleight-of-hand he'd learned as a street performer in Los Angeles.

"Don't try nothing funny," the pawn broker said. "I've got a sawed-off under my counter."

"Don't worry. I need this for personal protection." The Wasp pointed to the car in the parking lot. "I won that hoopty off a pimp in Memphis in a back-alley craps game. He might try to get it back."

"We're a long way from Memphis," the broker said.

"Pimp's can have long arms." The Wasp loaded all five bullets in the cylinder and snapped it closed. The pawn broker flinched, which gave the Wasp a secret leap of joy. "Who was that woman with the silver?"

"I've got no idea," he said. "She uses an alias and has only been in here twice. She always sells silver—thirty pieces of silver both times."

"She selling Jesus or something?"

"Would seem like it."

"Any idea where she's from?"

"Probably close by. She's not from this town. I figure maybe a couple exits up the interstate. She's probably too embarrassed to use a local pawn shop."

The Wasp nodded and walked out to the target range. He fired off the five shots, not aiming but taking enough time between each shot to convince the broker that he was actually testing the gun. With the barrel still hot, he emptied the cylinder of spent shells and loaded the secluded bullet, rolling the cylinder so it would be the first shot.

When he walked back inside, the pawn broker wasn't behind his counter. The Wasp looked around. No one moved in the shop. A twinge of paranoia crept up his spine. Any moment he would hear the thunder of a shotgun and feel the burning shot in his face. He kept the pistol by his side and crept farther into the shop.

He looked over the gun counter when he was close enough and saw the pawn broker's head jut from the register counter. The Wasp hurried behind the gun case. The broker lay on his back with his face toward the door to the storage area, one arm behind his back and the other at his side. The Wasp pointed the gun at the man in case this was an ambush. He prodded the broker with his foot. The man started to convulse. White froth erupted from the man's mouth. A half-eaten piece of red peppermint taffy lay near him.

The Wasp put the pistol in his pocket. He took a latex glove from his other and slipped it on. He grabbed the soft peppermint treat. It felt like any other piece of taffy. Then he smelled it. The old lady put a lot of peppermint oil in the stuff, but its aroma didn't hide the poison completely. He smelled the slightly acrid smell of the toxin she'd secreted into the treat.

"Clever girl," he said aloud. "I like you more and more."

A lady like her would work with poisons, because anything else would be too messy. He grabbed the remaining bag of candy from the counter and shoved the half eaten piece into it. He looked at the register and punched the no-sale button. The drawer popped open. Not much lay inside, but he shoved the bills into his pockets. The change stayed in the drawer. He didn't need that weighing him down.

The Wasp walked into the storage area. It was a fairly large room with shelves. Some things were covered with tarps. If he knew crooks like he thought he did, those were the items the pawn broker knew were hot and hadn't had time to sell. The Wasp found what he wanted in the corner. An old television monitor cycled through pictures taken by three different surveillance cameras in the shop. A VCR recorded the premises. He went over to this and hit the eject button. A RCA video cassette popped out. He took it and put it into the baggy with the candy.

"VHS? How quaint," he said back at the still-convulsing pawn broker. "You wanted someone to knock this place over and not get caught, didn't you?"

He walked back into the main part of the shop. A quick search of the broker's pockets found his keys. The Wasp pocketed these. He went to the gun case and took out the box of bullets.

"I can't let them think you were poisoned," he said back at the broker. "But pawn brokers get killed every day. There's a big city pimp's car in the lot, money stolen from the register." He pulled the pistol from his pocket and shot the man. The opposite side of his skull sprayed out a red mist. Blood oozed onto the floor. "And you've got a hole in your head."

The Wasp shoved the pistol back into his pocket. The warmth of it felt nice. His blood ran cold every time he had to use a gun to kill someone. It was so uncivilized. He needed to find the Silver Lady. They could do great things together, and she had a taste for peppermint, too. He was going to like Alabama.

Chapter Eighteen

Lily walked out of the kitchen when she heard the front door close harder than usual. Her sisters never slammed doors. Their father broke them of that habit seventy years ago. The old solid oak door fooled people with its weight, and the well-oiled hinges allowed it to swing closed with ease.

Two people stood in the parlor. She couldn't see them yet, but their whispers carried.

"If you've come about a room, come back here so I can get everything handled," she said stepping behind her desk.

A woman walked in followed by a familiar face. Vince Green had come back. Neither of the guests smiled. Vince looked stern. The woman appeared weary more than anything else. Lily smiled in hopes that it would change their countenance. It didn't.

"I never expected to see you again," Lily said.

"I hoped that I wouldn't have to come back here," Vince said. "We need two rooms."

"All right." Lily pushed a notebook across to him. "Sign in, and I'll get the other paperwork ready."

Vince scribbled his name. The woman wrote more legibly. Her name was Mary Carruthers. Lily glanced over her shoulder, embarrassed as she fumbled to find the legal forms. Nothing was where she liked it. The arrangement of items in the cubby hole of the desk told her that Tunie had had a hand in it.

"Tunie," she yelled. "Get in here."

The two guests flinched, apparently not expecting the power of her yell. Tunie hurried into the room, wiping her hands on an orange apron. She had her frantic look. Lily had left her alone for only a few minutes in the kitchen, but there was no telling what shape their supper would be in.

"You're back," Tunie said to Vince. "Did you find your daughter? Is this her? She looks a bit old to be your daughter."

"We didn't find her," Vince said. "That's why I came back

here."

"I'm Sara Beth's mother," Mary said. "My name is Mary."

Tunie stuck her hand out. "I'm Petunia Bellflower, but they call me Tunie."

"Nice to meet you," Mary shook her hand.

"Tunie, where are the check-in forms?" Lily asked.

"Are you two staying with us?" Tunie beamed. "Lucky we made so much chili."

"The forms, Tunie. Focus."

"Up there." She pointed to a pigeon-hole above a set of room keys.

Lily took down the papers. She smiled back at Vince whose look became more stressed by the moment. She pointed out where they needed to sign, which they did. He declared they would be staying indefinitely. This excited Lily. They might make a nice profit off Vince and Mary. Plus, he still owed them money.

"Rooms 2 and 4," Lily said, handing them the keys. "Tunie can show you the rooms."

"We can find them. Point the way," Vince said.

"Thank you anyway," Mary said, trying to cover his curtness with a veneer of politeness.

"That way." Tunie pointed to the staircase. "Third floor. Our rooms are on the second."

Vince thanked her and took Mary by the arm, leading her toward the staircase. Lily didn't know why he seemed so angry. He'd treated them like they had something to do with the disappearance of his daughter. The ruby necklace came to mind. He might think they stole it. No, that didn't make sense because he hadn't found his daughter to know it had been left behind. She wondered if maybe Tunie had somehow let him know. Perhaps, she'd come to her senses long enough to realize she'd stolen it and wanted to make amends.

"I'm sorry you didn't find your daughter," Lily said.

Vince turned as he ascended the stairs. "I've been to Tennessee twice and searched all the haunts of runaways. No one has heard of her. Then I went to Miami where I lucked up and found Mary after not hearing from her in 13 years. We also found Woodchuck."

"Oh, how is he?" Tunie interrupted with too much gusto.

"What does it matter?" Lily said. "He's telling a story."

"He was fine," Mary said. "He didn't know where Sara Beth was. He said you told him she'd gone to Nashville. Then he assumed she'd made her way home."

"I've heard about a serial killer in Tennessee. You don't think he might have wandered over to Nashville, do you?" Lily trailed off, realizing she had asked an inappropriate question.

"They found a victim that resembled her floating in the Mississippi River near Memphis, but it wasn't Sara Beth. Her trail went cold here. That's why I came back," Vince said. "If you don't care, I'd like to go upstairs and take a nap. Will there be enough chili for us?"

"Oh yes," Tunie said. "We eat around 6 p.m."

The two guests said nothing else. They ascended the stairs in silence. Lily finished filling out the forms after sending Tunie back to make a second pone of cornbread, something the poor thing could manage on her own.

Lily felt sad that Vince hadn't found his daughter. Deep inside, she hoped upon hope that nothing bad had happened to the girl, although while the self-styled Persephone Song had been with them, she'd thought the girl would come to nothing but a bad end.

***

Vince pulled Mary into his room. He sat on the single bed with a blue patchwork quilt for a duvet. She sat on the small armchair with velvet cushioning. The room reeked of old age and a bygone era.

"I thought you said there were three sisters," Mary said.

"There is another. She's the one who recorded that Sara Beth was going to Nashville."

"Where is she?"

"Apparently, they own a candy shop in town. I bet she's there," Vince said.

"I don't know why you think they are so sinister. They seem like nice little old ladies. Tunie is a bit on the batty side, but neither one of them seemed malicious."

Vince shook his head. "They aren't who I was talking about. The third sister, Camilla. She has an aura about her."

"Aura," Mary snorted. "I've been gone from California way too long for that kind of nonsense."

"Not that kind of aura. She gives off bad vibes. Her face looks like a permanent scowl. She always seemed on edge, like someone was about to reveal some horrible secret."

"You think she did something to our daughter? They have to be in their 80s."

"I don't think they did anything to her, but I think Camilla might have lied. If these are the guest rooms that everyone uses, there is a good chance Sara Beth stayed in one of them. Snoop around in yours and see what you can find. I'll do the same, then I'll need a nap."

"Why don't we ask Tunie which room Sara Beth stayed in? I bet she'd tell us," Mary said.

"I don't want them to get suspicious, especially Camilla."

"You're getting paranoid. You need to sleep."

Vince scratched his neck with far too much manic energy. She was right. He needed sleep. Paranoia plagued him in the past, but only during stressful times. As soon as he had a good night's sleep, it always went away.

"You're right," Vince said. "Let me catch some Zs."

"All right. I'll wake you for supper."

Mary left the room. Vince kicked off his shoes and laid out full length on the bed. Despite how dated it appeared, the mattress felt like a cushioning cotton cloud that would carry him off to the land of nod. He slid his hand between the mattresses, a habit he'd had since childhood.

His fingers rested in a hole torn in the top of the box springs. They touched a slip of paper in the metal springs. Vince got out of bed and pushed the mattress to one side far enough to see the tear. Instead of a ragged hole punched into the cloth, he found the cover had been sliced with a knife. His heart leapt. He might have found something hidden by his daughter. Mary had been right. Sara Beth could have stayed in one of their rooms. They had talked on the phone before she left. He told her he was headed that way. She knew that he'd eventually get to the Bellflower Inn. It made perfect sense for her to leave him a note. He plunged his fingers into the slit, and pulled free a piece of pink, lined paper folded into quarters. He unfolded it to full size. The writing rode across the lines with the slant of a left-handed writer. Just legible enough to read, the shakiness of the lettering suggested the author was old, sick, or in a hurry. It was not Sara Beth's writing:

This is my last will and testament. I, Jameson Quincy Slattery, known to many as Slappy, am dying. Been knowing this for a while. Can't drink like I have and bummed around without no permanent home or good doctoring like I have most of my life and expect to live long. I'll say that my last few days have been good. I caught a ride from a feller named Red out of Abilene, Texas. He drove for Road United number 1094. I ain't got an idea about his real name, but he could fart like a buffalo. Red brought me into this town before dropping me off. I've got 30 silver American Eagles that I've picked up along the way in a sock. Make sure he gets half of them for his trouble. Ain't much, but I ain't got much else to give. I want my remaining silver coins to go to Tunie Bellflower. She picked me up not long after Red let me out and brought me to her place. That lady took good care of me even when her sisters told her to toss me out on my ear. I couldn't get her to bring me booze, but every night I'd find a few pieces of peppermint taffy on my pillow before bed. I can't say they stopped the shakes, but they made life a little sweet. I hope the Lord is good to that woman. I hope that he can forgive me a lifelong sinner. If you find this note, you know that I took special care to hide it. Why? I don't trust Tunie's sister, Camilla. I've been on the road for nearly 40 years and seen a lot of buzzards. She's the one living in this house.

Vince saw the man's signature. Whoever he'd been, the sisters meant a lot to him. Vince started to feel bad about having such negative thoughts about them. He wondered if they knew about the will and the silver. Surely they would have found the sock when he died. They probably turned it over to the police. Once he woke up from his nap, he'd check for more holes to see if he could find the sock. He pulled the mattress into place and flopped down on it. Sleep came quickly.

***

Camilla walked into the shop from the back lot and took off her work gloves. After the trip down to the pawn shop, she'd decided to throw some more lime around the back of her store. It might keep any more complaints from going to the mayor's office. Eventually he'd send someone out to check for a sewage leak. No one needed to be poking around back there except her.

The kitchen smelled of sugar and spearmint. Rock candy suckers cooled in a stand. The green confection caught the light and made a stained glass pattern on the counter. She liked her spearmint suckers. The little pieces of candy looked like chipped peridot. Kids loved them too.

She walked to the sink and washed her hands. The clock above her head told her the rush hour was about to start. School had let out ten minutes before. The kids would be trickling in. She grabbed the spearmint suckers and moved them into the showroom. They took a place of honor by a pie stand that held bricks of peanut butter fudge.

As she stood ready for the children to pour inside, she noticed a thick envelope taped to the glass-topped counter. It peeled up with surprising heft. The writing on the top of it surprised her even more. It read: *To the Silver Lady.*

The door to the shop flew open. Three kids bounded inside. Camilla knew them instantly. They were her best customers: Timmy, Jimmy and Todd. She shoved the envelope into her apron pocket.

"Cool," Timmy said. "She's got the suckers."

"I love them," Jimmy said.

"Thanks for making them, Miss Camilla," Todd said.

"What else could I do for Huey, Dewey and Louie," she answered. "You asked for them, and I made them."

Each of the boys dug into his pocket and brought out fifty

85

cents. She took the money, and handed them each a sucker. They popped them into their mouths, made a sound of extreme pleasure, and then took them back out to relive the experience again.

"You boys want anything else?" she asked. "I made some fire balls yesterday. They're big enough to break your jaw and hot enough to make you spit fire."

They looked in the case at the giant, red candy balls but shook their heads. Their faces bore deep disappointment. She felt the same way. The mortgage wasn't going to be paid in fifty-cent suckers.

"Can't," Todd said. "They had the book fair at school."

"We spent all our money," Jimmy said.

"We probably won't be back until after allowance time," Timmy said.

"I'll keep three of them back for you boys," she said.

"Thank you," they replied in unison.

They bounded out of the store again. More kids came in. She knew all their names. It took a good thirty minutes to serve everyone. She wondered the whole time what was in the envelope. It felt like a lead weight in her pocket. The name bothered her as well. The Silver Lady implied that someone knew about her pawn shop visits. When the last customer left after the rush, Camilla stole back into kitchen.

The envelope looked like one of the cheap ones from the dollar store. The paper tore easily. A letter was folded so the message was turned outward, but something was wrapped inside it. When she unfolded the paper, it contained a large amount of dollar bills held together by a rubber band.

Black ink bled around the edges of the words and through the paper. The handwriting, precise and almost measured, gave her the creeps. The message didn't help:

Dear Silver Lady,

I watched you in the pawn shop today. We are kindred spirits you and I. The cool way you gave the pawn broker the poisoned candy after he hassled you. Take nothing off of no one is my motto. Apparently, it's yours too. Who would suspect the Silver Lady to be a killer? Not a single person. You are a true chameleon, living among the normies, watching them, preying on them when necessary. The way you presented him with that bag of poisoned candy was too cool for a virgin, but next time, make sure there isn't a video camera recording you.

Don't worry, Silver Lady, I took care of things. They'll never know it was you. I put a bullet into his skull and took the bag of candy away with me. The cops won't think to check for poison.

I hope you will accept my gift. I don't know what you need the money for, and I doubt that's enough to cover the debt. But more will come. I'm keeping my eye on you, Silver Lady. Think of me as your guardian angel.

Sincerely,

The Wasp.

Camilla almost dropped the letter. Not only did someone know about the silver, he claimed to have covered her tracks.

She peeped into the shop but saw no one. It was time to close up and head home. Her sisters would give her some comfort, even though she would have to make up some excuse for her strange behavior.

The hairs on the back of her neck prickled. If the bank wasn't determined to separate her from her sisters, this Wasp fellow was. She needed Lily and Tunie. If the Bellflower sisters had been separated at any time in her life, she would have withered up and blown away on the wind like dandelion seeds. Until right then, Camilla had only feared loneliness. The letter and its author now topped her list of terrors. The Wasp was somebody who thought he could extort something from her. What he didn't know is the only thing she had to give was her life. On the open market, it wouldn't be worth much.

Chapter Nineteen

The Wasp watched the Silver Lady leave her store like her hair was on fire and her ass was catching. His letter had freaked her out. That hadn't been his intention, although he knew if he were to receive a similar letter, it would send him into panic mode. It would make any predator feel that way. One as old as her didn't get to that age without being cagy.

He wanted to follow her but didn't want her to get wise to him. Maybe writing her a letter hadn't been the smartest thing, but he needed to communicate with her somehow. He knew she wouldn't go to the cops.

Now that he knew where the Silver Lady worked, he could find her with ease. The Wasp got ready to leave for a motel farther down the interstate. As he started to pull onto the street, a police cruiser rolled past. Two deputies sat in the car. Both looked like the local yokels that wore the badges in small towns like Jubilee. He hesitated. They parked in front of the Silver Lady's store. Both cops got out and walked up to her shop. This wasn't good. He wondered if they suspected her of something. The Wasp decided to run interference. It went against all his personal rules about dealing with authority, like *never approach a cop on purpose*. The Silver Lady needed him as much as he needed her.

He climbed out of his car and quickly walked down the sidewalk, arriving at the door of the shop after the police shook it. They gave him a side glance as he stopped beside them.

"Are they closed?" the Wasp asked.

"Apparently so," the cop with Jones on his name tag said.

With his hair swept up in a pseudo-pompadour and standing shorter than average, this cop looked like he would have the Napoleon complex. He wasn't black, but his complexion was much darker than the Wasp would have expected for this rural part of the country. He wondered if Deputy Jones might be a Cherokee or something. The Wasp had never scalped an Indian.

"Does this place always close so early? Seems like it would be bad for business," the Wasp said.

"The sign says she stays open until 5 p.m.," the cop tagged as Smith answered.

"I sure wanted some homemade taffy," the Wasp said. "I love good old-fashioned homemade taffy, especially peppermint flavored. There's not much of anything better. It makes me feel like a kid again."

Flaunting himself in front of these bumpkin deputies made him feel like a smart-alecky kid again, like a headstrong and cocksure teenager. It reminded him of the heady feeling from the first time he'd done it.

"She's pretty good at making taffy," Smith said.

The skeletal appearance of this officer made him look like he never ate anything, much less candy. Both deputies were cartoonish. Even their names seemed fictitious: Smith and Jones. The Wasp almost laughed out loud.

"You don't look familiar," Jones said. "Are you from around here?"

The Wasp shook his head. "I'm new to the area."

"Where are you from?" Smith asked.

"Out West."

"Why are you here?" Jones asked.

The Wasp threw his hands up and waved them in a jocular show of being overwhelmed. "I'm not a crook or anything. I came for work."

"There's nothing to do in Jubilee," Smith said. "We're lucky to keep this job."

"I don't work in Jubilee."

"Are you with the fair?" Jones asked. "We get a lot of unsavory elements that come along with it."

"I do some work for them," the Wasp said. "I get a lay of the land. Find out what's interesting and some local gossip. It helps the barkers. That's how I found out about this little sweets shop." He paused and gave the officers the eye. "Do I look sketchy or something?"

"Not really. You actually look a little too clean to be a carnie," Smith said, "but we're a bit on guard. A pawn broker down the interstate a few exits, near Milldam, got murdered earlier today."

"Do you think the owner here did it?" the Wasp asked.

"Miss Bellflower?" Jones asked with amazement. "Of course not. She's just a sweet little old lady who wouldn't harm a fly."

"She's the kind of lady who wouldn't even be seen in a pawn shop," Smith said. "We're here because the neighbors have been complaining about a smell from out back. The mayor sent us to look for a ruptured sewer line."

"The sheriff deputies check the sewer lines around here?" the Wasp asked.

"It's a slow day," Jones said.

"Even with a murder?"

"It's in a completely different county well out of our jurisdiction," Smith said.

"Come on. We'll ride over to Bellflower Inn and see if she's there," Jones said to his partner.

The police officers walked back to their cruiser. The Wasp stood looking into the shop as if studying what confections it offered. It would have been too suspicious if he hurried back to his vehicle. The cruiser stayed in place. The Wasp saw Smith poke his head from the car's window in the reflection of the storefront windows. He turned around.

"Something else, officer?"

"What did you say your name was?"

"I didn't, but its Graham Chapman," the Wasp said.

Smith gave him an odd look, and then screwed his eyes up like he was searching his memory to find where he knew that name from. "Like the guy from Monty Python?"

"My mother was Welsh and a big fan of the show. It was her luck to marry a man named Chapman, and my luck to get stuck with the name."

"I don't like Spam," Jones said in a falsetto British accent. "We used to get that show on APT. That's the public television station here in Alabama. I loved it, and the show with the lady who had purple hair. I don't remember the name of it, but she worked in a department store."

The Wasp faked a laugh, while his hatred of the two men began to seethe. "That was *Are You Being Served?* My mom liked it too. I guess I'm lucky she didn't marry a man with the last name Humphries."

"I'm free!" Jones said.

"See you around, Mr. Chapman," Officer Smith said.

The police cruiser pulled away with both deputies waving at him like beauty queens in a homecoming parade. He waved back, forcing his muscles into a smile to hide his revulsion. It was an easy feat he'd practiced over the years. He'd talked to cops many times, but these guys were the biggest rubes he'd ever dealt with, never expecting a serial killer to engage them in idle conversation.

The Wasp headed to his motel to spend the next few hours until the sun went down, and Jubilee rolled up her sidewalks. It would give him time to finish listening to the book on CD he'd picked up in Memphis. *The Girl Next Door* gave him ideas of new ways to torture his kills. He might try the burning-the-clit-off trick with one of his next victims. Then he'd come back and see what the Silver Lady, nee Miss Bellflower, hid behind her store.

Chapter Twenty

When Camilla walked into the house, the whole place smelled like food. Her sisters had made chili for dinner, and a lot of it judging by the smell. Her appetite had left her when she found the letter, but the smell tempted it back. Having seen a strange car with Florida tags parked on the street, she wondered if they had some new guest. Overcharging some out-of-towners might help make up the deficit on the month's mortgage.

Lily came into the parlor from the formal dining room with a big grin on her face, and Camilla knew it meant they indeed had guests. Her sister always looked so amazed that anyone would want to stay at their bed and breakfast. If the truth were known, it amazed her, too. The place was past rundown.

"We've got guests!" Lily said. "I was setting the table. They are going to eat with us tonight."

"I hope you're charging them for it," Camilla said.

"Why would I do that?"

"Because we're going to lose the house if we don't make money," Camilla said. "Giving away dinner isn't good business practice."

Lily looked a little miffed. "How much did you make today at the candy store?"

"Enough to cover the day," Camilla answered.

"Closing early won't help. Did you even get through the school rush?"

"Of course I did. What kind of stupid question is that? I sit in that store all day waiting for that rush. Today I had spearmint suckers. They are a hot seller."

"At a quarter a piece," Lily said. "You have no right to complain about me giving our guests supper."

"They go for fifty cents."

"Not much of a difference," Lily said.

Tunie bounded into the parlor like some kind of a wild

animal. The look of excitement couldn't be washed off her face. Camilla thought that her younger sister acted too much like a child, often forgetting the things she'd done and then lying about them. Sometimes those things were big, and those she never seemed to remember. Camilla always ended up cleaning up those messes.

"Did you hear?" Tunie asked.

"We've got guests that Lily isn't charging for dinner," Camilla said.

"Do you know who it is?"

"I don't care," Camilla said. "It doesn't matter because we're going to lose this place and have to live in the nursing home."

"It's Vince Green," Tunie said, oblivious. "He wasn't able to find his daughter in Tennessee or Florida so he came back here. I'm sorry for him not being able to find his daughter, but he was such a nice man."

Camilla's heart fluttered. The letter shoved into her pocket felt like lead weighing her down. Vince must be the Wasp. She knew he was watching her. He'd come to her shop and left the note, as though she walked right into his nest. She felt like an aphid waiting for the wasp's sting. He must know about everything. How he'd figured it out, she couldn't begin to guess.

"Are you okay?" Tunie asked. "You've gone all white."

Camilla tried to shake it off. "I'm a little tired. I think I got too hot at work making spearmint suckers."

"I bet you sold out in a flash," Tunie said. "The kids love those things. I bet Huey, Dewey and Louie were the first ones."

"They were, and the suckers flew off the shelf." Camilla feigned a bit more of her overheating. "I'm going to my room. I don't think I'll be down for supper."

"I'll bring you some up later," Tunie said and skipped back toward the kitchen.

As Camilla walked toward the stairs, Lily took her by the arm. Her sister looked less frustrated and more concerned.

"I didn't know you came home because you didn't feel well," she said. "I'm sorry I was short with you."

"Don't worry," Camilla patted her hand. "I'll be fine."

She hurried up to her room and locked the door. The bed felt good when she crashed onto it. Now she had to wait for Tunie to knock with her supper. Hopefully, her absence from the meal wouldn't rouse suspicions with the guests. It probably would, but she'd cross that bridge when she came to it. Maybe making the Wasp suspicious could give her an edge, although she felt unsure about what she could do with it.

***

Vince and Mary sat at the table with Tunie and Lily across from them. They all ate out of white bowls. Triangles of corn bread sat on white saucers. A plate of pickles and other sliced vegetables rested near a tureen of chili. A green glass bowl that looked like a sunflower held shredded cheddar cheese. Vince had never cared for chili, and the sisters' version was bland. It would fill his stomach for free, though. Since he needed to stretch his money as far as it would go, the free meal tasted like fiscal savings and hope.

"Where's Camilla?" he asked between bites of chili.

"She wasn't feeling well," Tunie said. "She said she got overheated at the candy store. Today she made spearmint suckers. The kids love them, but it takes a lot of time over a hot pot to make them."

"I was hoping to speak with her tonight," he said.

"She might be feeling better later on," Lily said. "Sometimes rest and a good meal puts the verve back into you."

"I hope so," Vince said.

"What do you want to talk to her about?" Tunie asked.

Vince felt like this poor old lady was trapped in a much younger frame of mind, as if something had stunted her emotional growth. He could imagine her still wearing poodle skirts and bobby socks. She got on his nerves.

"I wanted to ask her about Sara Beth," he said. "She was the last one to see her before she supposedly left for Nashville. I wanted to know if she noticed anything strange about her behavior."

"I was the last one to see her," Tunie said, "not Camilla."

"You're confused, Tunie," Lily said. "Camilla wrote the information in the book."

Tunie shrugged. "If you say so."

"Tunie has memory problems, sometimes," Lily said to Vince and Mary.

"I still want to talk to your sister, sooner than later," Vince said.

Mary patted him on the arm. "She'll be better by tomorrow surely."

He cut his eyes over at his traveling companion. "Our daughter's life is important to me."

"I love her too," Mary said, "but if Camilla is sick, then she's sick."

"I can tell by the way you left her with me and didn't come back for thirteen years, that's how much you loved *our* daughter.

"Who's ready for dessert?" Lily asked, getting to her feet. "Come help me, Tunie."

"I'm okay."

Lily lifted her sister's arm. "No, you're not. Come on here."

Vince watched the sisters leave. Sometimes his dislike of Mary couldn't be held at bay. The disappointment of Camilla not being at supper tore down most of his tolerance. That old lady was hiding something. Otherwise, why would she not want to be seen at all? She got wind that he was there and had avoided him. On the day he met her, she was as chatty as her sisters, maybe more so.

"There was no need for that," Mary said.

"Shut up." He felt no need to hide his frustration. "You've got no idea what I've been through to find *our* daughter."

A loud rap came from the door. He heard Lily hurry from the kitchen to the front. The floorboards creaked.

"How can I help you, Officer Jones?" Lily asked from the other room.

"I've got to go to the bathroom," Vince said.

He got up without Mary saying anything and hurried

upstairs. The rented bedroom looked less inviting now than the first time he walked into it. He felt like smashing up the place. It would make him feel much better, but the cops were downstairs. They were county cops, and he would be in deep trouble if he provoked those Southern-fried deputies. He'd seen too many old grindhouse movies about Southern prisons and chain gangs. So, he laid back and relaxed as best he could.

***

Lily heard one of her guests hurry up the stairs as soon as she let deputies Smith and Jones into the foyer. It had probably been Vince. His attitude needed a bit of an adjustment. She hoped that he'd excused himself upstairs to take care of it.

Deputy Jones looked flushed. Beads of sweat dotted Deputy Smith's lip.

"You two look like you need a drink of something cool and refreshing," Lily said.

"We've not got time," Jones said. "We stopped by to speak to Miss Camilla."

"There's been a big wreck out near the interstate. We had to respond to it before we got here. Is Miss Bellflower available?" Smith said.

Lily felt like the two deputies were the perfect partners. They almost finished each other's sentences like a married couple. She supposed working that closely with someone was similar to a marriage. Hers hadn't lasted long enough to get to that point.

"Camilla is not feeling well," Lily said. "She came home early from the shop today and has been in her room ever since. She wouldn't even come down to dinner."

"I guess that's why we missed her at the store," Smith said.

"Has something happened down there? No one has broken in, have they?" Lily asked, expecting the absolute worst. They had let the insurance lapse a long time ago.

Smith shook his head. "No, the shop owners beside the candy store have been complaining about a smell from out back. The mayor sent us out to make sure there wasn't anything wrong."

"Like a broken sewer line," Jones said.

Lily nodded. That sounded a little better than a robbery, but she couldn't figure out what would be causing a smell. Once she'd handled dessert with the guests, she'd head down to the store and check it out for herself.

"I'll let her know," Lily said. "I'll tell her to give you a call tomorrow so you can come and check. We want to keep the neighbors happy."

The two officers thanked her and left. She couldn't imagine what was wrong. If getting robbed was bad, having some kind of plumbing problem could be even more expensive. She wasn't going to bother Camilla with it tonight. She could go to the shop and check on it herself. Plus, she'd get the ruby necklace out of the safe and give it to Vince. That might put him in a better mood.

She got the impression that he was angry at Camilla. It occurred to Lily that he might have thought Camilla stole his daughter's necklace and then lied about her leaving for Nashville to cover it up. While that line of thought didn't seem logical, Lily found that in life, most people were rarely logical.

Her husband certainly had drunk himself to death without leaving her two pennies to rub together. He flushed her future down the toilet, making her an old maid at 22, and she hadn't been logical about never remarrying. As she stood in the foyer lost in thought, it occurred to her that Camilla had always been the most vocal in complaining about Lily's suitors. Lily caught herself twirling the strings on her apron. She dropped them and took dessert back to the dining room, so she could check on the shop before it got much later. Driving at night scared her, and the night would only get darker.

Chapter Twenty-one

The Wasp ate a nice supper at the restaurant near his motel room. He sat at the bar and waited for the sun to set. A baseball game was on the TV. He feigned interest until he thought the time was right to check out what the Silver Lady had in the lot behind her store.

The shops that flanked the Silver Lady's were closed. The sidewalks throughout the town looked like they'd been rolled up at dusk. The Wasp parked in the alley behind the row of old buildings. A privacy fence ran down the block of shops, making it hard to tell which was the Silver Lady's shop, but true to the word of the cops, something smelled foul. At the point where the stench made his eyes water, he climbed over the fence. Mostly hard-packed dirt made up the small area behind the candy shop. A pile of boxes covered with a blue plastic tarp lay three feet from the fence and about two from the door. The smell was strongest there. The Wasp knew what was under them.

The ground looked as if the Silver Lady might have been spreading lime to kill the stench. That worked best if you actually doused the body in it. He looked around for the shovel or sack of lime she'd used, finding neither. The back door to the shop looked heavy, made of steel painted glossy black. He wouldn't be able to kick it open, but the lock would be easy to pick, and she'd probably stored the shovel and lime inside the store.

The Wasp took his lock-picking kit from his back pocket and pulled on a pair of surgical gloves. There was no point in leaving fingerprints. The lock undid with little effort. The Silver Lady was lucky she hadn't been robbed before. He eased the door open, hoping an alarm wouldn't sound. When nothing did, he stepped inside and turned on the light.

The back door opened into a storeroom. Large sacks of flour and sugar lined several metal shelves. A yellow rolling bucket with a mop stood in the corner with a long-handle shovel propped beside it. A bag of lime, rolled at the top, sat on the floor. A small pile of white powder surrounded it. The Wasp grabbed the shovel and lime. He walked back into the space behind the store.

After clearing away the boxes, the soil underneath was disturbed like it had been recently dug up. It took only a few shovelfuls of dirt until he found a white sheet. The Silver Lady had buried the body only a few feet under the dirt. It surprised him that someone had not checked out the smell earlier. With the body uncovered, it became nauseating. He supposed she blamed it on the grease pit if anyone asked. That would have been his answer.

The Wasp reached into the shallow grave and lifted the body out. He laid her to the side and dug the hole deeper. Once he was satisfied the grave was deep enough, he covered the hole with lime, making sure to toss it up the sides. Then he pulled the sheet-wrapped body back into the hole. The covering slipped from the woman's face. If she hadn't already begun to decompose, and wasn't purple and slightly engorged, she would have been a pretty girl. He would have killed her, too. She fit the profile of one of his victims.

His mind began to wonder. What if the cops came back and found this girl in the ground? They would arrest the Silver Lady. He couldn't have that. They hadn't even met yet to compare notes. The Wasp was protective of his family, and she was now family. No one was going to take his grandmother down like that. He had the solution.

The Wasp reached into the hole and tore the sheet away from the girl. She was naked underneath. Just the way he would have done it. He reached into his pocket and took out a peppermint. Leaving the wrapper on the girl's stomach, he shoved the disc into her rectum as far as he could. The sphincter had set tight with rigor mortis so it didn't go far. The cold muscle squeezed like a python. He wiggled his finger in an attempt to loosen the muscle. When that didn't work, he pried at the sphincter with his other index finger. With that effort, his trapped finger came free. The stench nearly made him vomit. Rotting flesh had its own distinct odor, but putrid, trapped gas along with rotting flesh made a perfume he was afraid might have seeped through the glove and gotten onto his skin. The smell would cling like superglue.

The Peppermint Slasher's calling card would throw the cops off the idea that the Silver Lady had killed the girl. Why she chose to bury a victim behind the candy shop was still a problem. The cops might arrest her as an accessory to murder. He needed a plan. Busy work always helped him to think.

The Wasp removed his gloves and tossed them into the grave. He covered the body with lime and then with dirt. When he was done, the place looked like it had when he found it. Even the Silver Lady wouldn't know that he'd been there. He still had to clean up the mess in her storeroom. The only way to keep from being caught in a murder was to leave no traces. The labor gave him time to hatch a plan. It would solve the other issue he hadn't thought of: The girl wasn't slashed. His other calling card was carving his victims like a jack o'lantern. Giving the cops another M.O. might help broaden his profile, making him a harder target to find.

The Wasp slipped back inside. He took the mop out of the bucket, which still contained water that he used to mop up the lime on the floor. Everything looked tidy. He was ready to leave, when he heard a noise elsewhere in the shop. Someone walked toward him.

"Who's there?" the voice of an old lady asked.

He knew it wasn't the Silver Lady. Her voice had more pitch to it than this husky sound. The Wasp looked for something on the shelves he could use. He spied a box of large plastic bags. As the door to the storeroom opened, he grabbed one and secluded himself.

An old lady with steel gray hair poked her head inside. She looked around before stepping through the door. The Wasp didn't give her time to find him.

The bag went over her head. He held it tight around her face. She sucked in for air, but the plastic went into her mouth. Her arms flailed. He wrapped his arm around her. She backed against him, ramming her head into his nose. The Wasp felt the searing pain. He sniffed to check for blood, but none flowed or clogged his nostrils. His grip tightened around her more. The woman's breath increased. The faster she breathed the quicker she would run out of air. The Wasp felt her heart beat. It raced with her breathing. After what seemed far too long, she went limp.

The Wasp eased his grip on the bag. The old woman gave another hard buck. She flung her head back again. He was ready and avoided getting hit. His grip tightened around the plastic bag. The inhalation of plastic began again. It took less time for the effect to hit the woman. She went limp again. He held her up for a moment to make sure she wasn't playing possum. Although not quite dead, it wouldn't be long until she was.

He remembered why he didn't like strangling people. It took too much effort.

The Wasp laid the lady on the floor and searched her. He found a slip of paper in her pocket with three numbers written on it—the combination to a safe. Car keys were in the other pocket. A silver medical bracelet encircled her wrist. Her name was etched there: Lily Ann Bellflower Owens.

He studied the woman's face when he found the bracelet. It wasn't the Silver Lady, but he was sure this was her sister. He was glad the old bird hadn't slipped away just yet.

Chapter Twenty-two

Camilla sat in a wingback chair near the window with her feet propped on the matching ottoman, when she heard a light tapping on the door. Her empty dinner bowl sat on a TV tray to the side of the chair. She stopped her embroidery and looked up.

"Yes?" she asked.

"It's Tunie. Can I come in?"

"It's unlocked."

The door creaked opened. Tunie slipped in as soon as there was enough space for her to get into the room. She closed the door softly behind her. Camilla wondered why her sister seemed so secretive. There was no reason for the clandestine entrance to get the dirty supper plates.

"What is it?" Camilla asked, tying off the thread.

"It's late," Tunie said.

The mantle clock on Camilla's dresser said it was 9 p.m. Tunie stayed up much later than that. She preferred sleeping well into the day, like a teenager, instead of early to bed and early to rise. The news hadn't even come on yet, much less *The Late Show*.

"Why are you telling me about it?" Camilla asked.

"It's Lily. She's been gone a long time. Usually she's getting ready for bed by now."

"Where did she go?" Camilla asked, feeling real concern. Her sister rarely drove at night and only did so when there was no other choice.

"She went to the candy store. Some policemen came by and said they were worried about a smell from out back. She didn't want to bother you since you didn't feel well, so she went to check on it on her own."

"The smell?" Camilla couldn't hide her surprise. Fortunately, Tunie didn't notice the fear that tinged the question. "How long ago did she leave?"

"Hours. Sometime before 7 p.m."

"That's too long." Camilla got up. Her embroidery fell to the floor. "I need to go check on her."

"Why don't we call the police to go by there?" Tunie asked. "You don't drive too well at night either."

"I'll be fine. I'll drive slowly."

"Let me go with you."

"No, someone needs to be here with the guests."

Camilla didn't let her sister say anything else. She hurried as quickly as she could from her room and out of the house. Her car's headlights didn't help her night vision much, but she pulled onto the street and headed back to the shop. As she drove a million things ran through her mind. What would Lily find when she got there? Would she have already called the cops, or would she wait for Camilla? How would she explain it?

There was nothing she could do but tell the truth. Lily would have to understand. This wasn't the first time Camilla had to cover up things for Tunie. Lily had done it a couple of times, too, but it was always the small things she'd handled. Her elder sister never knew the true evils their younger sister committed. The girl in the grave owned a nice necklace. Anyone would have been tempted to steal it, especially a person who already had problems with reality and impulsiveness. Tunie heard Camilla and Lily talking about how the girl would sell the gorgeous thing for dope money or get her throat slit over it. She couldn't take the idea of some uncouth person profiting from it. In Tunie's mind, the only option was to kill the girl and to take the necklace. That would be Camilla's explanation if ever asked about the issue.

The old green Cougar that Lily and Tunie shared sat in Camilla's parking spot. She pulled in behind it. The shop lights shone onto the sidewalk, but she couldn't see her sister. At least the cops weren't around. Her sister had either not discovered the body in the back or was waiting for Camilla to explain.

Camilla got out of her car and walked to the shop's door. It was unlocked, and she went inside. Nothing stirred. She figured as soon as she walked in that Lily would come out from the back, wringing her hands. The place was too still.

"Lily?" she asked. Nothing moved. "Lily, where are you?"

She saw her sister's shoes when she rounded the corner of the glass display case. Inside the kitchen, she found Lily in a crumpled heap on the floor, her feet splayed out at odd angles. Lily's head rested in a pool of blood. The same stuff streaked down one of the counters. The corner of the cabinet hung with gore. Lily's vacant eyes stared up in silent terror. The ruby necklace rested in her open palm.

The air caught in Camilla's throat. For a moment, she suffocated on grief. Finally, a wail of intense agony tore from her throat. It burned as it exited. She'd failed to keep the sisters together. Another wave of agony hit her followed by a second wail. Once it escaped, Camilla composed herself.

She looked at the safe, still open. On the floor near the safe, glass from one of the jars of jawbreakers glittered in the light. The hard round candies littered the floor. Her sister had slipped on them. Lily, never good on her feet, had squatted down to get the necklace out of the safe and must have had a dizzy spell. She reached up to steady herself, toppled the jar, and then the rest was spelled out on the floor in her own blood.

Hot tears burned at the corners of Camilla's eyes. She needed to call the cops. Tunie would completely lose her mind, just like she had when their mother died. Another wail burst from her mouth. She steadied herself, looking back at the safe. A tent of paper was propped there.

Camilla stepped around the blood, careful not to trip over her sister or the jawbreakers. She took the paper from the safe. The writing on it looked all too familiar:

Silver Lady,

I'm sorry about your sister. I tried to help her, but it was too late. You can call the cops. Don't worry about the girl out back. I've taken care so that if they find the girl's body out back, you won't be a suspect. You'll find another note taped to the back door. It's what will get you off the hook. Consider yourself lucky. I rarely put my neck out for anyone.

Condolences,

She wadded up the paper and shoved it into her pocket. Vince hadn't written the letters. He would have made sure to have her and Tunie arrested for killing his daughter. She glanced back at her sister lying on the floor, looking more pitiful in death than she ever had in life.

The letter the Wasp promised hung on the back door. She opened it. It was a blackmail letter. It warned that if she told the cops about the body, he'd kill her and burn down her store. Whoever the Wasp was, he was confident in himself.

Camilla dialed the police.

***

Vince heard Tunie scream out. Her shrill voice woke him from a light sleep. In his dream, the scream had come from Sara Beth's mouth. Once he sat up in bed and collected his bearings, a feeling of relief washed over him. His daughter wasn't being murdered in his presence. Instead, one of the old ladies had screamed into the night.

Tunie wailed out again. Vince clambered out of bed. He pulled on a pair of pants and walked barefoot into the hall. Mary stood in her doorway looking at him. The sound of Tunie sobbing came from the parlor.

"What's going on?" Mary asked.

"I don't know."

Vince headed down to the parlor, taking two stairs at a time to check on the old lady. She might rub him the wrong way, but Tunie was like a kid. Once at the bottom of the stairs, he found Camilla and Tunie embracing each other on the beaten down antique sofa. Tunie buried her face into Camilla's bosom. Occasionally she'd rear up, sucking in great gulps of air between snotty sobs. Camilla looked at him. In the wan light cast by the floor lamp, Vince saw the tracks of tears down her checks.

"What's the matter?" he asked. "Is she hurt?"

Camilla shook her head and rubbed her hand on her sister's shoulder. Mary touched his elbow. She sighed. It was empathetic.

105

He had the impression she knew what had happened.

"Something happened to Lily?" Mary asked.

Camilla nodded. She kept her mouth closed, but tears dribbled from her eyes. Tunie let out another wail. It wrenched at Vince's heart. In that long, lonesome cry, he knew exactly what had happened. Lily was dead.

"I'm sorry," he said. "What happened to her?"

"She went to get this." Camilla held out her hand to Vince.

He reached out, and she dropped something into his palm. When he saw Sara Beth's ruby necklace, the one that matched the ring he'd pawned, his breath caught in his throat as he remembered the nightmare.

"Is that Sara Beth's necklace?" Mary said. "Where was it?"

"At my candy store in the safe. We found it not long after Vince visited us. We put it away for safe keeping," Camilla said. "When the police came about the smell at the store, Lily went to check it out herself. Apparently, she decided to bring this back. She knocked off a jar of jawbreakers and slipped on them. Lily had dizzy spells." She paused as her lips began to quiver. "She hit her head on the edge of the counter. It killed her."

"Lily! Why?" Tunie wailed out.

Vince closed his hand around the pendant. At that moment, he felt sorry for Camilla. She had probably found the necklace and decided to keep it for herself. Sara Beth was a runaway and a drug addict. He held no delusions about that. Old ladies the cut of the Bellflower sisters were savvier than people gave them credit for. Camilla probably thought keeping it for herself would keep his daughter from pawning it for heroin or methamphetamine. In her own way, she was trying to help the girl get clean. He made up his mind that was the secret she'd been keeping.

"It'll be okay," he said. "Mary, why don't you help Tunie to her room? I'd like to talk with Camilla."

Mary walked to the couch. She touched Tunie on the shoulder. "Will you come with me?"

Tunie looked up at her. She wiped her eyes with the heel of her palm and nodded. Mary helped her to her feet. They walked away, leaving Vince and Camilla alone. He sat down beside her.

"Thank you for giving this back to me." He held out the pendant. "You've no idea how much it means to me."

"I wasn't going to," she said. "Lily was the one with the scruples."

"I probably would have kept it myself. I know you were just trying to help my daughter."

"How is that?" Camilla asked.

"You took the necklace to keep her from pawning it for drugs," Vince said. "It was your way of helping her to say no."

"Is that what it was? Are you sure it wasn't pure greed?"

"Maybe, but I think it was more than that."

Camilla looked at him. Her eyes brimmed over with raw emotion. She began to cry. Vince let her put her head on his shoulder. Her glasses dug into the muscle, but he didn't ask her to move. She needed that shoulder. If he were to discover his daughter was dead, she would probably offer him the same. Maybe they were turning over a new leaf.

The old house moaned, settling on its foundation. Vince thought maybe the place cried for Lily as well. Camilla lifted her head.

"I lied to you about your daughter," she said. "She never told me that she was going to Nashville."

"Why would you do that?"

"She left with this shady man. I tried to stop her, but you know how headstrong youth can be."

"You've got no idea where they were heading?" Vince asked, a measure of anger and also hope building inside him.

"To trouble, I reckon," Camilla said. "I don't suppose it's got a ZIP code or cell phone service."

"I wish you'd told me the truth."

"I didn't want you to be disillusioned about your daughter. That Sunday I could tell how much you cared for her. Having faith in family is one of the only joys we have in life. I thought it was the right thing to do."

Vince shook his head. "I have no illusions or delusions about my daughter. You're right about both things, though. Family is one of the few joys in life, and if she left with some strange man, they were definitely headed for trouble. That's a place I've been to myself a few times. I hope it has a *return to sender* option."

He knew it didn't.

Chapter Twenty-three

The Wasp drove slowly down the dark back road. The only illumination came from his high beams and the moon, when its rays broke through the thick overhead canopy of leaves. The two-lane road seemed to stretch forever into the great unknown. Why he'd chosen this particular road had more to do with its romance than anything else.

The Natchez Trace was a Southern landmark that even he'd heard about in California. For some reason he'd always been drawn to it. An innate creepiness oozed from it. Apparently back in the olden days, outlaws traveled the well-worn path that the Indians had originally trod down. Now he blazed down it in the middle of the night, hoping that he would run into some luck. The cops had seen his current vehicle when he spoke to them at the Silver Lady's store. Although, they had no idea who he was, he didn't like that they might know how to find him. So far, his drive had been uneventful, with only a few passing cars going the opposite way. The Wasp began to think that he might come up dry and have to steal something from a truck stop—a crude but effective method.

He turned a curve on the dark road. The headlights revealed a motorcycle parked on the shoulder. No one milled around it. The Wasp slowed down and pulled in behind the bike. He kept the lights on and stepped out into the muggy night. Gravel crunched underfoot. He looked around, trying to spy where the rider might be.

"Hello?" he asked into the darkness.

"Yep," replied a deep voice.

Something about the voluminous sound that resonated from the trees sent goosebumps blooming up the Wasp's arms. He hadn't felt that in a long time. The last time he could remember being frightened was as a kid in a spook house on Halloween. That night the sudden roar of a chainsaw had brought the gooseflesh. The man's voice in the darkness sounded much like that old chainsaw from so long ago, harsh and rusty.

"Are you okay?" the Wasp asked back into the blackness.

"Yep. Needed to take a leak."

The underbrush started to rustle. The Wasp reached to the small of his back and touched the handle of his newest knife. His fingers brushed the hard plastic. It gave him comfort. No matter what kind of person emerged into the light, he could handle him.

A black man stepped out into the edges of the headlights. He smiled, looking pleasant and truly jovial. The Wasp felt at ease. This man would be a deacon in a church or maybe even the right reverend himself.

With a feeling of relief, the Wasp decided to have a smoke. He pulled the pack from his pocket, tapped one up, and put it to his lips. The smell of the butane from his Zippo lighter gave him a wash of memories like it always did, the smell of his first smoke after he'd killed his first victim. He'd been 14-years-old. The victim had been the prostitute who took his virginity. He'd paid her with money he'd stolen from a pot dealer at knife-point. The police never found her killer. They never even had a suspect. Back then, no one would have suspected a kid of committing such a heinous crime. That was a time before Columbine and other crazy white boys with guns.

"You smoke?" he asked the black man.

"No, I gave it up when I found the Lord," the man answered.

"I suppose it's a bad habit."

"It's sucking on the Devil's ding-a-ling, is what it is," the man said.

The Wasp choked on his smoke. He passed his hidden laughter off as if the puff hadn't gone down smooth. The other man shook his head as if proving his point. Smoke would no doubt be the devil's cum.

"That's a nice bike," the Wasp said, letting the cigarette hang from his lips as he walked toward the motorcycle.

"It's a fine machine," the man said. "I love riding it at night. It's like riding through God's own soul. The wind is sweet with the true fragrance of creation. The air is cool like when He walked in the midst of the garden. I can almost feel His hand on my shoulder."

The Wasp quit listening to the rambling man somewhere during the time he waxed about riding in God's soul. He nodded and studied the bike. Too much time had passed since he'd ridden one. He used to love them. There was a lot of freedom riding on the back of one. The deacon's red helmet sat on the saddle. The key stuck up from the ignition. Clean leather saddlebags straddled the beast. The Wasp kept nodding as he rounded the front of the machine. By the time he made it back to standing beside the deacon, the Wasp held his unsheathed knife by his side.

"What's your name, son?" the deacon asked.

"Why?"

"I want to say a prayer for you, so that God can grant to you the peace that passeth all understanding." He raised his hands to the sky and shook them.

"My name is Lucifer," the Wasp said. "The morning star."

The deacon's hands dropped, and his joyful facial expression fell as well. "Son, that's not something to be joking about."

"Who's joking?"

The deacon didn't have time to answer. The Wasp slit his throat across the front. The only sounds the deacon uttered were gurgles as blood poured into his lungs and spurted into the night air. The man tried to punch him, but was too shocked to land a decent hit. He gave a valiant effort, the Wasp thought, shaking his head as he stabbed him in the stomach until the deacon fell to the ground.

Once the other man was down, the Wasp did a proper job of giving him an ear-to-ear gape. While the other man was still conscious enough to appreciate it, he carved a smile on his face and a swastika on his forehead—just for fun. When the Mississippi State Police found this man, they'd think the Klan had gotten hold of him.

The Wasp sucked off another of the devil's ding-a-lings while he waited for the deacon to die. Once the other man was with his creator in the cool of evening, he dragged him back into the woods.

"You better hope I didn't get poison ivy dragging you back here," he said to the dead body. "Otherwise I'm coming back and cutting off your ding-a-ling and shoving it in your mouth. See what St. Peter thinks of that."

The Wasp went to his vehicle. He removed the keys and the license plate. They would drown along with his new knife in the nearest creek with deep enough water. It felt good to kill the deacon, not as satisfying as slashing a woman, but good enough. Pious people should enjoy being murdered. It got them to their eternal goal quicker.

He climbed astride the motorcycle, pulled on the dead man's helmet, and headed into the night. With the visor up, the Wasp smelled the sweet air heavy with honeysuckle and what he thought might be magnolia blossoms. So, this felt like riding in God's soul? He gave out a hearty laugh and gunned the throttle to feel the raw power of the engine and the unbridled wind blowing against him. *This* was like riding on a demon's back.

Chapter Twenty-four

A tin cracker box with rust around the bottom lay on Camilla's bed. The upturned lid held a stack of black and white photos. More snapshots lay in three different piles on the bed. A round hat box rested on the floor near Camilla's feet. She hadn't yet scratched the surface of all the photographs she had of her life. The small stack of pictures she held had been bound with an old piece of kite string. The first image told her what the rest would be. The fifteen photographs were from the time she and her sisters had entered the town's homemade kite contest in 1961.

She thumbed through them, wishing they had been colored prints. The bright and vibrant hues of the varied kites looked like nothing but various shades of gray. Her memory of them wasn't much better. The only kite she remembered well had been their own. Tunie insisted on entering the contest. She and Lily thought it was too silly. Neither of them had ever liked kites as kids, but their baby sister had. She wouldn't talk about anything else but the kite contest. Finally, Camilla convinced Lily to enter. They had made a candy-striped kite. It flew well, the tail fluttering in the wind with little red and white flags hanging from it. Their brother was still alive back then. She happened upon a picture of him smiling and holding the string of their kite. A cigarette dangled from his mouth, and his daughter, their only niece, clung to his leg as if he might fly away.

Now that Camilla let her mind wander to that day, she remembered that Gordon had told Suzie that if the wind got strong enough, it might lift him up like the kite. A smile crossed her thin lips. It was a pleasant feeling. She had spent too much of her time over the last several hours crying. She put the picture of Gordon and Suzie on the middle pile.

The next photo was of Lily. She looked sad and happy at the same time. The kite contest wouldn't have been long after her husband had died. Her older sister still wore her wedding ring.

Their niece sat on the statue of an elephant that used to be in the town park. Lily held onto her to make sure she didn't fall off. Suzie beamed with a smile.

Camilla put the picture in a pile of photographs where Lily took center stage.

Someone knocked on her door. Lost in thought, Camilla barely noticed. When it finally dawned on her that she'd heard a knock, she said "come in" with little more than a broken whisper. The door opened. Vince pushed his head inside.

"Am I bothering you?" he asked.

"No, I was going through some old photographs. The mortician said that they do this thing now at funerals where they show a bunch of pictures of the deceased. I didn't want to bother with it, but Tunie insisted. It was easier to give in to her. Otherwise, I'd never hear the end of it."

Vince stepped inside and closed the door. He sat on the edge of the bed. The tin box fell over but none of the piles of pictures were disturbed. He clutched a folded piece of pink paper in his hand. A worried expression creased his face. At least, Camilla thought it looked like worry. She had trouble telling anything about this man's facial expressions. He was a strange duck, as Lily would've said.

"I've heard of them doing that," Vince said. "I never go to funerals so I have no idea what it's like."

"What brings you in here?" Camilla asked, putting the few remaining pictures on her lap.

"I found this the other day in my room."

He handed her the paper. She unfolded it and read the shaky handwriting as his eyes studied her. She remembered the bum who had written the note. He had been a nasty man who Tunie had dragged up from somewhere. She'd insisted that they take him in and help him out. Camilla remembered the silver coins as well. They were what she'd pawned the other day when that letter-writing kook had seen her.

A paranoid thought entered her mind. Although she had dismissed the notion of Vince being the Wasp, his giving her the last will and testament of Slappy the Bum might be his way of saying he knew something.

"I remember him." She folded the paper and dropped it behind the pile of Lily pictures. "That man didn't have a pot to pee in, as the old saying goes."

"So there aren't any silver coins hidden anywhere?" Vince asked.

"I would highly doubt it. Tunie dragged that character up, harping on Lily and me until we let him stay. He died in his sleep, probably from the DTs." Camilla shook her head. "We had to deal with the most red tape you'd ever seen because of that bum. It was the last time we let Tunie drag up any more vagrants. That girl will never learn."

"What's the matter with Tunie? Something seems not right about her," Vince asked.

"That's because something isn't right with her. She's stuck in her teenage years." Camilla thumbed through the photos on her lap until she found one of Tunie and a young man. She showed it to Vince. "That's Robert. He was Tunie's boyfriend and supposedly her fiancé. He left her for no reason, and she never heard from him again. It broke her heart."

Vince took the picture and studied it before handing it back. "That was a long time ago."

"She never got over it."

"But she's old now. Why couldn't she move on?"

"When Robert left, something snapped in her brain. She'd always been a bit on the squirrely side, but that was the straw that broke her." Camilla put the picture on the first pile.

The rest of the photographs went onto that pile as well. She picked up the hat box and took the lid off, revealing a few colored prints. The first one she picked up was from sometime in the early 1970s. Each of the sisters wore identical dresses in different colors. They looked hideous with their hair piled high on their heads. Steel gray already streaked her hair. Laughter escaped from her.

"Look at this," she showed it to Vince. "I can't imagine why we ended up old maids."

"Neither can I." Vince sounded like he was humoring her. Camilla knew that was exactly what he was doing.

She put the photo on the end pile with the others for the slideshow. "Tunie does things…"

"What kind of things?" Vince asked.

"All kinds of things, but mostly devious. She'll take something from a store and not pay for it, but then she doesn't remember doing it. Lily and I have had to take back a lot of stuff or cover up for her."

"She's that bad off?" Vince asked. "I knew she was peculiar, but that is far gone. She isn't dangerous, is she?"

Camilla paused as she looked at another photograph. "Not usually."

"But she has been?"

She huffed a laugh and looked at Vince square in the eyes. "We've all been dangerous at some point, Vince."

In the depth of his eyes, she saw that he wasn't trying to beguile her. He was being genuine. His eyes darted to the floor. The eye contact was too much for him. Sometimes she was more intense than she remembered.

"I suppose that's right," he said.

"Your daughter's necklace…"

"What about it?"

"Tunie stole it. Lily found it where she'd hidden it and brought it to the store where we could keep it safe. Apparently, Tunie remembers this, that's why she's taking Lily's death so hard. She feels responsible."

"She told you that?"

"Of course not, but I've known her for a lifetime. You pick things up along the way," Camilla said.

"You just keep covering up for her?"

"Yes. I have no choice, especially now. If they put Tunie somewhere, I'd be all alone, Vince. I've spent my life trying to keep us together. There is nothing worse I can imagine than being alone. All hopelessly alone. If they took Tunie that's where I'd be."

"I'm sorry," he said.

"If you don't mind, I need to finish looking through these." Camilla looked back to the pictures.

Vince stood and left. She didn't bother watching him out. Memories started to flood back into her mind. This mingled with the trepidation about her future. The piles and boxes of photographs held moments of her life. Now, those images were the only thing she had to remember Lily. In a room full of memories of happy times, Camilla felt lonely, and knew that was how she would feel for the rest of her life. The years would become a constant misery. The pictures fell from her hands to the floor, and she slammed her balled fists on the mattress over and over until the piles of photos fell over and mingled together. All of her organization was ruined, but she didn't care. Nothing mattered anymore except the deep and aching loneliness.

Chapter Twenty-five

The Wasp sat in the third pew from the back on the left side. A fleshy woman in a large black hat sat beside him. She smelled like gardenias and musk. His nose burned from the stench, which also made his eyes water. That was a good thing. It made him look like he was in mourning over Lily's death. People were crammed in the funeral home chapel like sardines in a can. He had no worries about the Silver Lady recognizing him or even seeing him. She had many well-wishers at her sister's funeral. He'd blend in.

The undertakers did a good job covering up the gash in Lily's head. He cut it with his knife and fractured the skull with the mallet the Silver Lady kept at her shop. Luck favored him in that situation. Lily had still been alive when he crushed her skull so she bled like she'd hit her head on the counter. The police hadn't bothered with an autopsy.

The thrill of killing without the fear of getting caught carried a certain appeal, but he thought that making his victims look like accidents lacked the palpable thrill he loved so much about murder. If he started working with the Silver Lady, the Wasp might have to get used to that kind of rush—one that tasted a lot less like peppermint and more like vanilla.

He watched the Silver Lady interact with another old woman, probably her other sister. The Silver Lady wore dark blue instead of black. She removed her glasses at the beginning of the service and left them hanging around her neck on a silver chain. A white handkerchief kept her eyes free of the tears. Her sister bawled the whole time. At moments she wailed louder than the preacher could speak. He paused to let her braying die down to a whimper so he could continue.

On the pew behind the sisters, a man who looked rather nondescript patted them on the shoulders. The Wasp hadn't gotten a good look at his face, but he didn't resemble the sisters.

He might have been an in-law.

The woman with him looked like she'd been ridden hard and put away wet one too many times. The Wasp had seen that look before, during his years of wandering around committing brilliant acts of violence. She'd spent too much time sucking on a bottle and a lit cigarette. Her face told him that she was no stranger to harder things as well. The clothes she wore told him she was in *recovery*. She would use words like *closure* and *dependency* in everyday conversations. That woman would think that everyone was in *codependent* relationships. For that alone, he'd love to kill her. Recovering drug addicts loved psychobabble and pseudointellectual discussion. They always reminded him of therapists he'd encountered in his life. He'd always wanted to kill those tin-plated Freuds as well. An opportunity never arose to fulfill that completely conscious desire.

"Lily Bellflower Owens, 84, was born on June 26. She married her only husband, Ernest Owens, at age of 20. He died two years later from a heart attack. Her love for him was so strong that she never remarried. Because of this, Lily never had children. Her love was lavished on her only niece Suzie Gates nee Bellflower by her late brother Gordon. She and her sisters, Camilla and Petunia, loved their community and church," the preacher read from the obituary. "She would wish this not to be a funeral but to be a celebration of life."

The Wasp wanted to amen him, but this would draw unnecessary attention. So he kept silent as he sat on the pew, strangely enjoying the funeral of one of his victims. It never crossed his mind to attend a victim's funeral. The idea of watching the loved ones mourn made his balls tingle a little bit.

His cell phone vibrated in his pocket. He slid it out. A text message waited to be read. He hadn't gotten a text in a long time. Being a chameleon meant having few contacts. Before he even looked at the message, he knew who the sender was. His *sister* decided to make contact. This fool of a girl was flat broke not far down the road in Birmingham. The text had been short but laid out her need for his help.

The Wasp sent a message back. He told her that by a stroke of luck he was near the city and would meet her that night. She sent the name of a bar, probably a dive where a bunch of drunks and addicts hung out. He told her he would meet her around 9 p.m.

He smiled while the preacher talked about the glories of heaven and the preciousness of God's love. The Wasp nodded his head as if he agreed. The god of murder was precious as well, and he seemed to be working the machine in the Wasp's favor. This god demanded a sacrifice like the wrathful God of Moses. The Wasp didn't have a fattened calf, but he did have a first-born sister. Surely a sacrifice such as that would be pleasing to the gods. He almost chuckled thinking about it, but caught himself and kept nodding woefully.

Chapter Twenty-six

Vince and Mary sat across the table from each other. It was the same restaurant where he had stiffed the waitress the first time he'd come through the town. He'd picked the place because his conscience had bothered him ever since then. Mary had mentioned that whenever that happened, the establishment took the cost of the meal out of the waitress' salary. Servers made a meager salary at best with tips to supplement the rest. The poor waitress who'd served him and the Bellflower sisters that Sunday looked like she needed all the money she could get, so he planned to leave what he owed plus a large tip. He didn't care if it pulled too hard on his remaining cash. Lily's death had put things into perspective for him again. Being a good human was as important as reuniting his family. For too long he'd used his desperate search for Sara Beth to justify his poor behavior.

"Why didn't we stay with Camilla and Tunie and eat the food they have at the house?" Mary asked. "We're kind of strapped for cash."

"It seems that all that was brought to the sisters were buckets of fried chicken or casseroles. I'm not keen on either one," Vince said. "Plus, I have another reason for being here."

The waiter walked over. He took their drink orders. Mary got a diet soda. That was how she ordered it. Vince had noticed while spending time down South that almost everyone called every brand of soda *Coke*. He almost ordered a soda the same way but decided on something different. For some reason, sweet tea sounded like the nectar of the gods. The waiter took down their drink orders and headed to fill them. Mary looked over the menu. Vince knew what he was having.

"This shrimp po' boy looks enticing," Mary said.

"As long as you know we're going Dutch, it's the best thing on the menu," Vince said.

"I wouldn't think of letting you to pay for my meal," she said with frostbite in her words. "You harbor a deep grudge toward me, don't you?"

"Why wouldn't I? You abandoned us. If you had been around, maybe Sara Beth wouldn't have gone off chasing after some drugged-up jam band."

Mary put her menu down. "I have had to deal with a lot of things while I've been in recovery. One is guilt. I wish I hadn't left, but to be honest, if I had stayed, we would have probably taken off after that band together. I was an addict when I left, whether you knew that or not. I would have probably drawn her into my world sooner than when she found it."

"I knew you were an addict," Vince took a sweating glass of tea from the waiter. "I had to run off a few of your dealers before you left. I remember getting rid of one gentleman I can only describe as a pimp."

"They called him Rico the Parrot," Mary said. "I remember that day."

"I'm glad you didn't bring me hepatitis as a present," Vince said.

"I'll come back in a moment," the waiter said, trying to excuse himself.

"We're ready," Vince said. "I want a grilled chicken Caesar salad with the breadsticks please."

"Shrimp po'boy," Mary said. "Separate checks. I'm his recovering addict of an ex-wife not worthy of his paying for my meal. He's outstanding at holding grudges."

The waiter took their orders and hurried away as quickly as he could. Vince knew the boy had to be no more than 16-years-old. He'd probably started the job to earn money for a car and wanted no part of two old people arguing about a pimp named Rico the Parrot.

"That was embarrassing," Mary said.

"They were facts," Vince said. "You did a pretty good job of embarrassing yourself."

"Facts of my past are what I have to accept every day. It's part of the program. I don't need you to throw them back in my face. Believe it or not, in the last twelve years, I've changed. I'm a better person who almost has her life together. Maybe when we find Sara Beth, I can get all the pieces back in place, even the broken ones. Time and maturity are almost as good as superglue."

"Camilla lied about Sara Beth going to Nashville," Vince said.

"You've been harping on that since Memphis."

"No, she told me last night. Apparently, she didn't want me to lose respect for my runaway daughter. Sara Beth left with some shady guy, according to Camilla. She doesn't know what happened to her."

"That means she could be anywhere," Mary said.

"She was lying again," Vince said, staring at nothing in particular.

"Is this another bout of paranoia, or do you have facts?"

"Not hard ones, but some definite soft ones."

"Like what?"

"Tunie killed her." His words fell like lead. He thought about that idea many times since his conversation with Camilla, but voicing them hurt like they had been weights dropped on his head.

Mary looked as if she'd been bitten by a snake. The utter disbelief on her face appeared almost comical. Vince knew she had difficulty believing it.

"Tunie's not right," Mary said, "but there's no way she could do anything like that."

"Camilla said that Tunie went crazy back in the '60s when her fiancé left her. She said that Tunie does things and doesn't remember doing them."

"That doesn't mean she'd killed Sara Beth."

"She stole her necklace. Camilla said that she and Lily covered up a lot things that their sister did. I think she was trying to tell me my daughter is dead."

Mary shook her head. "That would mean that Camilla was an accessory to murder. Why would she do that?"

The waiter came with their orders. He put the plates down and hurried away. They had definitely freaked out the kid.

"She cared about her family like we do. She would do anything to keep them together and apparently has. Lily and Camilla covered up that Tunie had stolen the ruby necklace. They kept it in the safe at their candy store once they realized what had happened, but you can't think for a moment they would have expected to give it back," Vince said. "Camilla didn't condone the murder. I don't think she is that kind of lady, but she covered it up to keep her family together."

The tangy sauce on the salad popped in Vince's mouth. They said nothing else while they ate. Mary stared at him, but he tuned her out and thought about his daughter. She was dead and buried somewhere Camilla knew about but wouldn't tell. He couldn't blame the old woman too much, because he would have done anything to protect Sara Beth—and at one time even Mary. Vince was no superman, having been a CPA before taking off to find his daughter. CPAs didn't take on drug dealers and pimps for fun, but he had been motivated. Old Southern ladies didn't hide hideous crimes without a reason either, but he would try to convince Camilla to tell him where Sara Beth was buried. If he promised not to tell the police, she might help.

He wondered if the smell Lily had gone to investigate might be the body of his daughter. Maybe she'd been trying to cover it up because she was in on it, too. As he chewed the last piece of chicken from the salad, he decided he would approach Camilla tomorrow night. She needed the night of her sister's funeral to grieve. He could give her that before making her grieve for the other sister.

Chapter Twenty-seven

As the Wasp had expected, the bar where he was meeting his sister was a dive. The thing he hadn't anticipated was that it was a gay dive. He didn't even know those places existed. Every gay bar he'd wandered into had been swanky. Leave it to his sister to find a place like this. It was located in the basement of a building without current tenants. Brown paper covered all the windows of the stores above. No windows pocked the black walls of the bar. Can lights hanging from the ceiling provided the only light in the place except behind the bar. Several strands of clear rope Christmas lights surround a large mirror. Two fluorescent fixtures hung above the bar as well. A few round tables and straight-back chairs sat along the walls. The main floor was left for dancing or other libidinal activities.

After walking around the perimeter of the place, he determined his sister hadn't yet arrived. That too was like her. She was never on time. There had been too many lessons to teach the girl, and she had failed to learn any of them.

The Wasp sat at a corner of the bar facing the walls, which were mirrored, affording him a view of the entire place. There was little to worry about. No queer would be making a surprise attack.

"What can I get you?" asked the bartender with a large handlebar mustache.

"A Shirley Temple."

"I haven't had one of those queens ordered in a while," the bartender said. "I don't even know if I can remember how to make one."

"Try," the Wasp said.

The bartender walked away. He waited for both his drink and his protégé. The drink arrived first. He sipped it through a straw. The liquid got lower and lower in his glass. The bartender came back to check on him.

"Another one?" he asked.

"No, I'm driving," the Wasp made it sound as serious as he could.

The bartender laughed. It was genuine, something the Wasp hadn't expected. Most of the time bartenders had a smart comeback for his absurd answer.

"You are the living end," the bartender said. "A big strapping fellow like yourself orders a Shirley Temple and then tells me you're driving and can't have another. You aren't one of those Christian missionaries who come into places like this and try to pray the gay away are you?"

The Wasp gave the man the eye. "Do I look like someone who would pray about anything?"

The bartender studied him. The Wasp felt like the man's eyes were probing him all the way into his soul. He felt naked and vulnerable at that moment. If the examination didn't stop, the bartender might find himself dead in a back alley before the night ended.

"You look like you might prey on someone, instead for someone," the bartender said. "You're looking for someone, aren't you?"

"You're insightful."

"We get a lot of people looking in this place. They're mostly out for love in all the wrong places," the bartender said.

"That's how the cowboy got shit in his mustache," the Wasp said.

"Probably on Brokeback Mountain," the bartender said without missing a beat. "Who are you looking for?"

"My sister. She said that she would meet me here. Do you know her?"

"What's her name?"

"She goes by a bunch of them, but Candace is the one she uses the most. Tiffany is another of her favorites. Her real name, however, is Amanda," the Wasp said.

"Those are all common names. What does she look like?"

"Average height, a little underweight with short black hair, unless she's wearing a wig, which is always a possibility."

"She must be a drug addict or a prostitute," the bartender said.

"Probably both."

"Is that her?" The bartender pointed to the door.

The Wasp looked around. In the dim light, he recognized his sister. She looked rail thin and wore a lopsided blond wig. All the tell-tale signs of drug use were there. Loathing rose throughout him until he thought it might make him burst.

"That's her," he said.

The bartender whistled and walked away. His sister saw him and made a beeline for where he sat. Without saying anything, she sat down beside him and waved the bartender back over. She gave her order, PBR. The bartender brought back a sweating can of the stuff before a single word passed her lips. The whole time the Wasp plotted what he would do with her. She was now a huge liability besides a giant nuisance.

"Thanks for coming," she said.

"What else was I going to do? You said that you were in trouble."

"I've gotten myself stranded here," she said. "I've been here so long I'm getting a drawl and starting to like Pabst Blue Ribbon."

"How did that happen? I taught you how to get out of any situation from any place."

She looked over at him. "I ran out of money."

The Wasp watched her in the mirror behind the bar. He didn't want to look her in the face.

"How is that? You stole a lot of money from me."

"Expenses. It's not cheap traveling across the country."

"Don't lie to me, Amanda," the Wasp said. "I taught you how to lie, and I can tell when the poisoned words fall from of your lips."

"I spent it all on drugs. Is that what you wanted to hear, M—

"Don't say my name, or I'll stab you where you sit."

"Not in the middle of this bar," she said. "You're not that dumb."

"There's not a queer in this place who would pay attention to some skank bleeding out on the floor. This place is about anonymous sex. That's why you picked it so that no one would pay much attention to us. So far, no one except the bartender has, and he might not make it through the night."

"Are you going to help me out?"

"Are you clean yet? Don't lie."

"No, I got some stuff on credit," she said.

"Hand job or hummer?"

"That's none of your business."

"Why did you leave, Amanda? Why did you take off with my money and risk everything? We were going to be a team that would go down in legend like Bonnie and Clyde, or those two kids who went on that spree through the Badlands."

"None of those teams came to good ends," she said. "I didn't want to go out in some blaze of glory. I decided that living into old age sounded better."

He grabbed her wrist and squeezed it, hard. The skin only covered her bones. There was little cushioning. She flinched from the pain.

"People like me don't make it to old age because of the old adage *you live by the sword, you die by the sword.* People like you don't make it to old age because of the saying, you live by the needle; you die by the needle."

"I haven't been using needles. I've never been an IV user."

"Finish your beer, we need to get out of here," he said.

"Where are we going?"

"Hunting," he said.

"Goody."

The Wasp knew that she was lying about that. Her voice lacked any of the enthusiasm she had once had for being part of the chase. She finished off the beer, and he left a few bucks on the bar. They walked out together.

The city smelled like diesel fumes and barbecued pork. The sound of the traffic on the interstate sang in his ears. The Wasp led his sister to the stolen motorcycle. They climbed on, and he drove them through the streets of Birmingham. The foot and street traffic was steady. It made it hard to find a good location. Finally, he saw a dark area past the downtown university. A small empty lot with no lights. He pulled into it and killed the bike.

"We aren't going to find anyone out here," Amanda said, getting off the motorcycle.

"I know that," he said, "but I haven't t seen you in a while."

He started kissing her on the neck. She tried to pull away, but he gripped her closer to him. He hoped she struggled a little. It made him all that much happier.

"I don't want to do this," she said.

"It's not optional," he said. "You stole money from me. The only way you are going to be able to pay it back is through submission to my every whim"

"I said no." She pushed him back.

The Wasp stumbled backward on purpose. She didn't have the strength to fight him off, but he wasn't going to let her know that. It would take the fun out of things. He smiled and moved back in. She slapped him across the face. Rage started building up in him along with a sexual thrill. He grabbed her and pulled her to him again. His mouth pressed close to her ear.

"You don't have an option. I only do two things for pleasure, this and the other thing."

He felt her shudder beneath him. She went soft and let him begin kissing on her. Before long, she stood naked in the night air. Her body was little more than bones with tightly stretched skin. She had lost any attractiveness she'd ever had. Sores were crusted on her back and buttocks—a sure sign of methamphetamine abuse. The stupid girl should have known he wasn't going to risk catching something from her.

The Wasp walked behind her. He pressed himself against her, so she could feel his erection in her ass. She gave a fake moan of pleasure. It didn't faze him. Neither one of them was being honest. He reached around her with his left hand and cupped her breast while reaching for his knife that he'd secured to the saddle of his bike. His mouth pressed to her ear again.

"You like what I've got for you?" he asked.

"Yes, give it to me."

"Beg."

"Please let me have it. Give it to me good," Amanda said.

"If that's what you want."

His left hand shot up and pulled her head back by her hair, while his right hand pulled his knife across her throat. She tried to struggle, but the deed was done quickly. He'd opened her throat from ear to ear. She didn't last long. He let her crumple to the ground.

Nothing of beauty was left in her. He saw a withered hag so addicted to meth that track marks lined her breast like rivers on a map. She'd stolen his money and worse, his trust, something he'd given away only once or twice in his entire life. She got what she'd deserved, but not quite.

He bent over and carved *Silver Lady* into her chest, a message he knew would be understood by the police as if written in thirty-foot glowing letters. The Wasp walked to the motorcycle and took a towel from the saddlebag. It was from the cheap motel where he'd been staying. He cleaned off her blood from his naked body and shoved the soiled towel into a garbage bag before stuffing it back into the saddlebag. He fished a peppermint from the pocket of his pants that lay on the ground, unwrapped it and walked back to Amanda's body. It took a little more effort than he'd expected to shove it inside of her, but the medical examiner would get a minty surprise when he opened her up and found his calling card hidden away—higher than usual. It would be something that sawbones would never forget. The Wasp knew that his name would live forever like his idols Jack and Zodiac. By the time it was all over, Charles Manson would be less famous than him.

The Wasp dressed and rode off into the night to find a lonely road with a convenient bridge over a deep creek to toss his bloody towels. His *sister* lay where she'd died, waiting to be found in the morning when he'd be safely back in Jubilee.

Chapter Twenty-eight

Vince walked along the banks of the creek that ran through Jubilee. The city had built a nice walking park that followed it a ways until it made a big bend. The smell of the loamy earth of the banks filled him with renewed energy. The day broke off hot for the time of year. At least he thought it broke off hot. He'd never spent much time in the Deep South. The heat wasn't as oppressive as the humidity. It didn't make sense to him why so many men wore heavy sports coats and suits to the graveside yesterday. He'd worn his only remaining button-up shirt and had sweated through it.

All the trappings of Lily's funeral had weighed heavy on his mind. Vince had spent the night before in fitful sleep, dreaming about his own daughter's funeral. Most of the day had been spent trying to get the image out of his head. By the time sunset rolled around, he'd found the park and hoped it might ease his mind.

The sun set. It cast an orange glow on the ripples of the water. The humidity still hung heavy in the air, but the heat of the day cooled into the evening. Sweat beaded on Vince's back. A drop of it slipped all the way down to his buttocks. He sat on a concrete bench underneath a magnolia tree and looked out over the water. His mind wouldn't wander. He wanted it to, but it kept looping back to Sara Beth. The burial made him sad not because of the loss of Lily, he'd barely known her, but because it made him think of his daughter, at best lost out there in the great big world, but probably rotting in some shallow grave.

The last time he'd seen Sara Beth was the day she left with Woodchuck. They'd fought. He disapproved of Woodchuck so much that it caused her to rebel against him by going with him. Some of the daydreams he'd suffered from that hot day were the remembrances of her leaving to follow that jam band. Vince had never talked with Woodchuck until Miami. Their interaction had been mainly through glances and windows. Woodchuck never stepped foot into his house, and he never made an attempt to reason with the boy. Sara Beth's leaving was all Vince's fault. He knew this. If he'd only done things differently, the whole story of his life and hers might have been changed. However, "might" was an awful big word. He knew that dwelling on *mights* helped nothing. It was akin to *woulda, shoulda, coulda*. Although he tried to get lost in the beautiful sunset, his daydreams came back.

"I love him, Dad," she had said in her grown woman voice, but to him she still sounded like a little girl.

"No, you don't. You don't understand what love is. You're too young."

"I'm 18-years-old, not a little girl," Sara Beth said. "Don't worry we're only going to follow the band through California. I'll be back in three months."

Before he could reason with her, Woodchuck blew the horn of his SUV, and she shot out the door. He watched her ride off to follow a band with a bunch of drugged-up neo-hippies. Vince convinced himself that she would come back before they made it to San Francisco. The next time he heard from her four months had passed, and she was in Manitoba, Canada. When his pleas to come home fell on deaf ears, he went after her.

At that moment, he sat staring out on an Alabama creek that rolled swiftly by. Her trail had gone cold here. Woodchuck and his group had quit following the band months ago after New York City left them worse for wear. They'd been wandering around doing drugs and living the bum lifestyle.

He'd followed them all that time, always a day or two behind. The things he had done to keep himself alive embarrassed him.

A bird sang sweetly in the tree above his head. It was her last song for the day. He knew that she would soon bed down. The birdsong trilled high and sweet. It lulled him so his mind could wander away from the thoughts of his daughter that had so plagued him all day he thought he might lose his mind.

All this cracked down the middle and disintegrated into the rumble of a motorcycle riding down the dirt path. The sound of the engine thrummed through him. It vibrated his teeth. This wasn't a dirt bike some kid was hot-dogging. It was a man's bike. The sound of the engine told Vince it was a Harley.

The single headlight shone from the dusky dark. It grew closer and closer until it almost blinded him. The bike and rider came to a stop in front of him. Vince could see the guy well enough. He had short cropped brown hair and a strong jaw line. The guy put down the kickstand and stopped the motor. He climbed off and walked toward Vince.

"Good evening," the biker said with a lively voice.

"Evening," Vince replied.

The man sat beside him. "This is a nice park."

"I thought so when I found it," Vince said.

"You don't sound like you're from around here," the man said. "I hoped you were a local yokel."

"Sorry, only been around a few days."

"You might still know. Do they let you sleep in the park? I can't find any campgrounds I trust pitching my tent in. There are some fish camps on this creek, but I think I heard banjos. You know what I'm saying." He elbowed Vince in the ribs.

The guy beside him seemed a little too chummy, but Vince knew exactly what he meant. The whole place wreaked of molesting hillbillies, although everyone he'd met so far had been nice.

"I doubt they will let you sleep here," Vince said.

"Nuts." He put his hand out for a formal introduction. "I'm Graham Chapman."

Vince took his hand and shook it. Graham Chapman couldn't have been much older than 32 or 33. "Like the guy from *Monty Python*?"

"My mom was a big fan. That's why I'm out riding the road on my hog. Mom died a month ago from breast cancer. I'm riding across country in her honor." Graham pulled back the leather coat he wore to show a pink T-shirt with an awareness ribbon printed on it.

"Sorry to hear about your mom," Vince said.

"Thanks. So what's your name?"

"Vincent Price Green."

"Vincent Price, huh?"

"My mom was a big fan of his," Vince said.

"Help me! Help me!" Graham said in a high-pitched voice. *"The Fly."*

"Excellent movie."

"So, any motels around here? Cheap preferably."

Vince shook his head. "The only place I know of is where I'm staying. It's a bed and breakfast owned by some old ladies, but I don't know if they'll take on anymore guests right now. One of them just passed away."

"Can I follow you back there? Nothing wrong with trying."

"Sure, let's go now. I'm getting hungry."

Vince led Graham down the path back to the parking lot. The biker walked his Harley, and they chatted. When Vince climbed into Mary's car, Graham started up his ride. They drove into the growing night.

***

The house felt empty as Camilla sat alone at the breakfast table. Tunie had already gone to bed even though the sun had just gone down. Mary was in her room, and Vince had gone out and not yet returned. Camilla toyed with a tuna casserole someone from church left for them. Of all the casseroles, tuna was her least favorite. She never quite understood why people thought that those in mourning wanted something so disgusting. It beat fried chicken. They'd been given several buckets of the stuff.

Lily had liked casseroles. Tuna was one of her favorites. In all their years, the three Bellflower sisters had been separated only a few times. At those times it was always Lily who left. The first time was when she'd married. When her husband died, that brought her back to Camilla and Tunie. The second time was to take a job in Indianapolis, but the big city was too much for her. The third time was a brief stay in a nursing home after a knee-replacement surgery. Camilla didn't know if that counted, because she and Tunie visited her as often as possible. The older sister's death was the fourth and last separation. Somehow Camilla thought they'd all go together. She'd planned it that way. When one of them—probably Lily because she had been the oldest— got deathly ill, Camilla had planned to poison Tunie and then herself. All the sisters would die on the same day and rest beside each other until the great day of reckoning.

The door opened. From the breakfast nook, Camilla saw Vince walk inside. A young man followed him. The stranger looked handsome and rugged with a slim frame. He wore motorcycle leathers. Vince said something to the man that she couldn't hear.

"Miss Bellflower," Vince said loud enough for her to hear through the hallway. He walked toward her with the man in tow. "This young man is named Graham Chapman. He needs a place to sleep."

Graham Chapman smiled at her. His eyes were a dazzling blue. His teeth were artificially straight, no doubt from braces worn as a kid. A day's growth of beard covered his strong chin. He almost looked like a pirate. She knew he wasn't, but Camilla Bellflower knew a rogue when she saw one.

"I understand that this is a house in mourning," Chapman said, "but I would appreciate being able to let a room for the night."

Camilla smiled at him. "Let a room for the night? Where did you learn that phrase, Mr. Chapman?"

The rogue's smile wavered enough for her to notice.

"I don't know," he said.

She took a drink of the store-bought sweet tea sitting beside her half-eaten plate of casserole. "I don't know if my sister and I are up to it."

"I'm pretty tired of riding. I've been going for a long time. Can I pitch a tent in your back yard? I don't feel like riding until I find a place," Chapman pulled a wad of money from his pocket. "Money is no object."

Camilla looked at the roll of greenbacks and then back at the man's beautiful eyes. "I suppose for one night, if you don't mind

Kentucky Fried Chicken for breakfast."

"Is there any chance I can get some supper?" Vince asked.

She nodded. "There's a lot of chicken. I was having tuna casserole, but it's self-serve."

"I understand. Has Mary eaten yet?"

She shook her head. "She said that she would wait on you. I suppose I'm not good company right now."

Vince nodded and headed upstairs. Camilla stood and pointed Chapman back to the desk area. She went behind the desk and got the book.

"Name?" she asked.

"Graham Chapman."

Camilla cut her eyes over the top rim of her glasses. "Real name."

"Graham Chapman. I promise it's my real name. My mother was a big Monty Python fan."

"I don't know who that is, but I know a fake name when I hear one. Worst is you've used a famous person's name. I suppose you do it to build quick rapport. You're a conman, aren't you?"

"It's my real name. Mothers do name their children after famous people." He pointed toward the stairs. "His name is Vincent Price Green."

"I'm not sure that's his real name either. His daughter came in here under the name Persephone. Even better was she was traveling with a red-haired fellow named Woodchuck. You can put your fake name in the fake book, but in the real one, I need to know who you really are."

All the politeness and cleverness fell from Chapman's face. Something hard like granite overtook it. His eyes darkened with a seriousness that almost took Camilla's breath away. The man's face was now one of a gargoyle not a human.

"You know who I am," he said in flat, forceful tones. "Do you like the taste of peppermint?"

The epiphany clicked in her brain like a light switch. "You're the Wasp."

He smiled a malevolent smile. "And you're the Silver Lady.

We have things to talk about."

"I ought to call the cops," she said.

"Why? Feel like turning yourself in?"

"No, I feel like turning you in. There's probably a reward for you. I don't want to end up with a slit throat. If you remember, I didn't kill that girl. Your note says so. I didn't do it in the first place. I just buried her."

"You've got nothing to fear then. I'm not going to slit your throat because I consider you family, and I hold that higher than anything else. There's no need to lie either. I consider murder a positive trait in a person."

Chapter Twenty-nine

The Wasp sat across the round breakfast table from the Silver Lady. He ate the sympathy tuna casserole. It felt good to eat something homemade. His insides filled with warm feelings of hominess. Although the Silver Lady hadn't prepared it with her own hands, he knew that she could make something as wholesome.

Vince and his companion, Mary, sandwiched him in. The Wasp didn't like the woman. She made him want to kill her. Everything about her screamed addict. She was the older version of his preferred target. A leathery lizard like her would be easy to kill but satisfying.

"I heard on the news that the police think the serial killer who leaves a peppermint in his victims might be in Alabama," Mary said.

"The Peppermint Slasher," the Wasp said, sounding as nonchalant as possible.

The Silver Lady looked uncomfortable when he said that. He hadn't revealed that he was the Peppermint Slasher, but she knew. The clever old broad knew many things. She was the cat that ate the canary after poisoning it with peppermint taffy.

"That's the name they called him," Mary continued. "Apparently, the authorities in Birmingham—is that right?" The Silver Lady nodded. "They found a mutilated body near a university. She had a peppermint inserted into her anus and a name carved into her stomach."

"Who's name?" the Wasp asked, feigning morbid curiosity but thoroughly enjoying the open discussion of his own deviance.

"Silver Lady."

The Silver Lady strangled on the brownie she ate. As she coughed, Vince reached out to slap her on the back, but she held up a hand.

"This is a dry brownie," she said. "I'm okay, but could we

change the subject? I am in mourning. Plus, murder and mayhem aren't appropriate dinner table conversation."

"She's right," Vince said. "Graham, we're here looking for our daughter. You've been out and about on the roads of this great country of ours. You wouldn't have seen her by any chance. I know it's a long shot.

The Wasp smirked. "I've seen lots of daughters. What does she look like?"

Vince brought out the well-worn photo of a pretty girl the Wasp instantly recognized. She was the body buried behind the Silver Lady's shop.

It was everything he could do not to laugh out loud when he saw the Silver Lady squirming again. To be so coldhearted and sly, she didn't handle discussion of her dalliances well.

"I saw someone who looked like her not that far from here. It was a couple of days ago over in Mississippi at a big truck stop near Jackson," the Wasp lied.

"Really?" Mary asked.

"She said her name was Persephone. I was pretty sure that was a fake name. She was trying to hitch a ride with a trucker named Red. I'd met him in the greasy spoon at the truck stop. He said he was heading to San Jose or one of those San places back in Cali. There's a ton of them, too many to keep track of."

Vince looked at his companion. They both had a wide-eyed expression of renewed hope. They thought their daughter was heading home.

The Wasp looked at the Silver Lady. She'd steeled herself again. Now, she was a stone-cold granny.

Vince and Mary had gone to their rooms. The Wasp followed the Silver Lady through the house like a child following his mother. They stood in the kitchen. She scraped leftover tuna casserole into a scrap bucket she kept under the sink. He took the plates and put them in the sink.

"What do you want from me?" she asked after spending a long time in silence.

"Nothing," the Wasp answered back.

"Why have you been sending me letters?"

"I feel like I've found a long-lost relative," he said. "The first time I saw you in that pawn shop, it was like looking at my grandmother."

The Silver Lady finished scraping off the last plate. She put it in the sink herself. "Your grandmother?"

"I didn't know my grandmother well. My parents moved around so much and weren't the best people in the world. They were both disowned by their families."

She plugged the sink and began running hot water into the basin. A squirt of liquid Joy filled the air with the scent of lemons. Suds formed in the water. She took a few of the plates and submerged them.

"I hope you rinse plates better than you lie." She plunged her hands into the soapy water.

"You see what I mean," he said. "It's like we have a psychic link. I've been killing people for years, since I was a teenager. No one has ever suspected me."

She passed off a washed plate. "You're lying again."

He rinsed the plate off. "Okay, I've never been arrested."

"That I would believe, but you still haven't answered my question. Why me? I'm a little old lady who didn't want my sisters to know we were so desperate for money that I had to pawn silver coins."

"Who's lying now?" he put the rinsed plate into the dish drainer.

"I don't know what you mean."

The Wasp looked at the Silver Lady, her expression still steely cold. Like him, she'd been hiding her true nature a long time. He'd read a story in high school about a landlady who liked to stuff pets. She also liked to poison tenants. The Silver Lady reminded him of that character.

"I kill because it's a need I have, like eating or sleeping. Without it, I get physically ill," the Wasp said. "Why do you do it?"

The swinging door to the kitchen opened. Another old lady walked in. A sudden burst of butterflies filled up his stomach. He'd been talking so freely, thinking that no one could hear. The Silver Lady had put him at that much ease. Her sister carried in a dirty dinner tray. She looked depressed but not surprised. He knew that she'd either not heard them or already knew about her sister.

"Thank you for bringing me supper," the sister said to the Silver Lady.

"I'm glad you ate." The Silver Lady nodded her head toward the Wasp. "This is a new guest we've got for the night. His name is Graham Chapman. This is my sister, Tunie." She nodded from him to her sister.

"Hello," Tunie said.

Before he could answer, she left.

The Silver Lady handed him another plate to rinse, which he did. She smiled at him apparently reading his mood, and said, "She doesn't hear well. Plus, when she's depressed, she walks around in a near stupor. That's when she does the things she doesn't remember, like killing people or poisoning candy." She paused and gave him a deep look. "Don't worry though, no one knows who you are except for me."

"Can I trust you, like I think I can?"

"We have each other by the short hairs. If I tell on you, you tell on me. I haven't killed a soul, but I have been covering up things Tunie has done for decades"

The Wasp thought of the saying that there was honor amongst thieves. In a world of murderers, there was trust in mutual paranoia.

"I've done what I've done to keep my family together. Tunie kills because she sees something she wants," the Silver Lady said.

"What did Vince's daughter have that she wanted?"

"The ruby necklace you found in my safe. That girl would have pawned it for drug money." The Silver Lady shoved a plate at him.

"I remember your sister Lily holding it in her hand."

The Silver Lady looked at him with a stare that pierced to his core. She pulled the plug in the sink, leaving dirty flatware in the water. The vortex made a loud sucking sound, as though all the joy in the room swirled down the drain. She walked away, leaving him standing there, holding a damp dish towel. He almost laughed at the absurdity of it.

Chapter Thirty

The annoying beeping of his watch's alarm roused Vince from his sleep. The glowing numerals read 1 a.m. He dressed and left the Bellflower Inn within half an hour after waking. One of the sisters would find the money he'd hidden under the pillow. It would take care of his bill. Mary was on her own. He needed to get back to California as quickly as possible. If Sara Beth showed up at home and he wasn't there, she might leave again. Then he would never find her.

The empty asphalt rolled into the darkness as he merged west on the interstate. Mary's car was a junker, too old for a cross-country drive, but he had no choice. No one would pay anything for her car, so getting another set of wheels would not be possible.

The stars shone bright in the night. Vince stared at the Milky Way in the clear velvety sky. He loved the stars. Sara Beth had too. He remembered that cartoon about Fievel, the Russian mouse. It had a song about how people who were separated could look at the same sky and be together. At that moment, the thought gave him comfort. Somewhere out there, his daughter stared at the same sky and loved him. The image made him push the gas pedal harder. Time was wasting away too quickly for Vince to worry about the speed limit.

***

An insistent banging on the front door awoke Camilla from her sleep. By the time she'd gotten into the hallway, all the others in the house were awake. Tunie stared out of her door. Her face bore her depressed stupor. When Camilla got to the parlor, she found Graham standing in the shadows. He looked ready to pounce on whoever stood on the other side of the door. The glint of a metal blade caught her eye. He meant business.

"It's okay," Camilla said as she passed by.

"I'm here just in case."

A peep through the windows flanking the door revealed a

sheriff's deputy she didn't recognize on the porch. He knocked again.

"Miss Bellflower," he said. "I need to talk to you."

"Hold on." She unbolted the door and pulled it opened.

The deputy stepped inside. Camilla took several steps back to keep from falling as he did so. Graham stepped up and put his hand on the small of her back to stabilize her.

"What is it?" she asked.

"The police have found something at your store," he said.

A knot of dread tightened inside her. They'd caught her. Steeling herself as was her way, she stood up straight to him, giving Graham a pat on the arm for helping her.

"What is that, officer?" she asked.

"A body."

"A body?" Tunie said from the other end of the parlor.

Camilla knew her sister's hearing problem came and went according to how scandalous the gossip was. She saw Mary standing with Tunie. Their faces were slack with shock.

"Of a young woman," the deputy continued as if there had been no interruption of his news.

Camilla felt her knees go weak. Graham steadied her again. He pushed her toward the parlor.

"Maybe you should sit down, Miss Bellflower." He slipped his mouth near her ear and whispered. "Don't worry about yourself or *Tunie*. Remember the letter."

"I think I need to," she said going along with Grahams' charade. The way he said her sister's name told her that he hadn't believed the story about Tunie's episodes. She felt like that made him unpredictable.

Camilla sat in one of the wingback chairs. Tunie and Mary sat on the sofa, and Graham sat in the other chair. The deputy kept standing. He looked around the room with one hand resting on the large, black flashlight holstered on his belt next to his pistol.

"They are guests," Camilla said, indicating Graham and Mary. "We have a third, but I guess he somehow didn't hear you knocking on the door."

"You said it was the body of a young woman," Mary asked. "What did she look like?"

"We've got her at the morgue over in the Milldam Hospital. I was hoping that Miss Bellflower might be able to enlighten us on who she is," the deputy said.

"I don't know anything about it," Camilla said.

"Apparently, you knew something about the smell," he said. "The reason the police were in the back of your lot was because the mayor had complaints. He said he even talked to you about it. You told him it was the grease trap."

"I remember that, and I thought it was," Camilla said.

"Are you sure?" the deputy asked.

"What else would I have thought?" she answered. "Why should I have thought a body was buried back there? Sometimes animals fall into the grease while looking for a midnight snack. I can't tell you how many 'coons and possums I've pulled out of that thing. It's a death trap for small vermin."

"My daughter is missing," Mary said. "Could this woman be her?"

"I don't know," the deputy said, sounding a little upset that Mary dared to ask him a question.

"I'm going to get Vince." Mary stood and headed upstairs.

"Are you arresting me or something?" Camilla asked.

"We believe that she is a victim of that serial killer who's on the loose," the deputy said.

"Why do you think that?" Graham asked.

"We found a peppermint candy inserted inside of her."

"Why would he bury her behind my store?" Camilla asked.

"We don't know," the deputy said, "but the body had been there a while. Are you sure you don't remember anything suspicious?"

Camilla felt Graham willing her to spill the beans about the letter. Under the circumstances, it was time. She let out a long sigh.

"I knew the body was there," she said, "but I don't know who it is. All I know is that when I went to the store a few weeks ago, I found the lot behind the place dug up.

"Why didn't you alert anyone?" the deputy asked.

"There was a letter stuck to the back door," Camilla said. "It was from this Peppermint Slasher fellow who everyone has been talking about on the news. He told me that he'd used the back of my store to bury one of his victims."

"You didn't think the police should know?" Tunie asked.

"He threatened me in the letter and Tunie, too. Threatened all of us." She looked at the deputy and thought of her dead sister until tears burned in her eyes. "I'm an old lady. We're both old ladies. I was—*am*—terrified. Imagine if you were as helpless as we are and some deranged killer threatens you. You'd do anything to keep him away, even keep a murdered body a secret. I guess I shouldn't have left the body there, but I had no choice, all things considered. You have to see it my way. What protection could the police offer? No one knows what this killer looks like. He could be in this room right now for all we know."

"It's okay, Miss Bellflower," Graham said. "You did what you felt you had to do for your and your sisters' safety. That killer is probably a desperate criminal who would do anything to stay free."

"Do you have the letter?" the deputy asked.

"Of course," Camilla said. "Do you think I'd be stupid enough to destroy the only thing that could keep me out of jail for murder?"

"Please get it for me," the deputy said.

Mary hurried down the stairs. She looked frantic. "He's gone."

"Who's gone?" the deputy asked.

The tension Camilla felt from all the focused attention finally broke. A rush of relief washed over her, but she knew it wouldn't last long.

"Vince, my ex-husband. He's gone and stolen my car. It's our daughter who's missing," she said.

"Do you think that he might have killed this girl?" the deputy asked.

"Of course not!" Mary screamed. "He's been chasing her for a year trying to keep something like this from happening? What kind of question is that?"

"How about y'all? Do you think he might be this killer?" he asked the others.

"We don't know him that well," Camilla said.

"What does your car look like? I'll put out an APB," the deputy said to Mary.

Camilla listened to Mary describe her car between bursts of tears as the knot in her stomach eased. She looked over at Graham, who gave her a wink. She gave him a small smile back. His plan had worked so far. She and Tunie might stay together after all and not in a jail cell. Graham was the only person who could ruin the setup. Chances were that he wouldn't do that. Like Graham said, he was a desperate criminal bound to stay free, so he could keep on killing.

After the police left and everyone went back to bed, Camilla sat in the breakfast nook drinking a cup of coffee. Under normal circumstances, she'd never have caffeine at this time of night, but there was no way she was going back to sleep anytime soon.

The floorboards creaked. She knew who crept along the hallway. It had taken him longer to come than she'd expected.

"There's some coffee in the kitchen," she said when Graham stepped into the light.

He sat down beside her. "I don't drink coffee. I won't have trouble staying up. Most of my waking hours are spent at night."

"Now what?" she asked.

"I've spent my whole life covering my tracks. They don't have a single good picture of me and only general descriptions." He took her hand as a grandson would his grandmother's. "Plus, I've met some of this place's crack police officers. We're safe."

"They won't call in the FBI?" she asked.

"They may, but as old as the *murder* is, they'll look on down the road for me. Remember, I killed a woman in Birmingham the other night and left a lot of calling cards. They'll start looking for me there. You act like you haven't been doing this kind of thing for a while."

"I have never done this. All I've ever done is take care of Tunie's messes. Unlike you, I've never taken any particular pleasure in any of it."

Graham narrowed his eyes. "Don't act like you're somehow better than me. You've killed people like I have. We're one and the same."

"No, we're not," she said. "I don't know where this idea that I'm some kind of geriatric angel of death came from, but I'm nothing like you."

"We're exactly the same, and we're joined at the hip now because if you turn me in, I'll turn you in," he smiled again. "I'd like a job at your store."

"Ain't going to happen."

"Why not?" His face became serious again.

"There's not going to be a store. The police will keep it closed to look for clues. Plus, I already have so few customers. After all this, everything will dry up and blow away."

"They won't keep you closed for long. There's not anything to find. The murder happened so long ago, and I assume at another location. *Tunie* wouldn't have lured that girl to your shop, would she? The cops will scour the back lot and maybe the storeroom. They've already done a sweep of the kitchen area after your other sister died. They'll know it's clean for this murder since it obviously happened long before Lily hit her head."

"Having you around complicates things. I'm getting too old for this game. The only reason you found the girl was because I've been slipping in my old age. I've never forgotten to put lime on a body, but the shallow grave was a bad idea. I've never killed a single person, but I've disposed of plenty of bodies."

She *had* disposed of many bodies. The old men she'd gotten all those silver rounds off were buried deep beneath the back shed. No one ever smelled a thing, even in the dog days of August.

"Why do you even need the shop?" Graham asked.

"I can't pay the mortgage on this place. Tunie and I need a place to live. We can't make the back payments. We'll be out on the street at the end of the fair coming up."

"How much do you owe?"

"Over $10,000 in one lump sum," Camilla said, knowing that to many people that was not much money. "That's only the house mortgage, not including the rent on the store and various other bills that are so far behind I'll never get them paid before I meet my maker."

"I've got that much in my boot," Graham said.

"Are you offering it to me?" she asked.

He nodded his head. For a moment, she though he might be taunting her before deciding to do her in. Death no longer scared her, but she'd read about his gruesome methods. She knew Graham liked to carve on people while they were still alive. He got a thrill from the kill, the thought of which caused her stomach to knot up.

"It won't come free," he said. "I want to do a job with you. We need to work together on a great scheme I have. It'll make us more famous than you could ever dream."

"I don't want to be famous," Camilla said.

"Sure you do. The draw of infamy is why we kill. We'll be like Harold and Maude," Graham said.

"They were lovers, not partners in crime," Camilla said. "I thought you said that I was like your grandmother."

"You are, but that doesn't mean anything. I was training a girl I called my sister, but we were lovers too," he said.

"Let's keep it professional," Camilla said, feeling dirty at that moment. "Emotions come with their own set of problems."

"You're right. That's something you've taught me," Graham said.

She had him. If everything went down the tubes, there was a weak point she could exploit. The young man thought of her as his grandmother. It scared her to imagine what ideas he'd formulated about her before they'd met, but if it came down to it, Graham would kill to protect her. He'd be killed doing the same thing. When the bus barreled down on them, she'd make him throw himself in front of it. One might call it murder, but she thought of it as self-defense.

Camilla patted his hand like she would have her own grandson. He smiled and laid his head on her shoulder. Something maternal switched on inside her. He wasn't going to be that complicated. The boy might be a godsend. The fear of being alone niggled at her so hard she couldn't think straight. Graham could take Lily's place. Tunie wouldn't care because he would be excellent at cleaning up her messes. Camilla would never have to be alone.

"You're a sweet boy, Graham. My sweet boy."

Chapter Thirty-one

The flashing blue lights pulled Vince out of the mental fog he'd been driving through. His head cleared when he realized that the officer meant for him to pull over. The car shuddered over the ruts paved into the shoulder. A police car pulled behind him and extinguished its bright headlights. The blue strobes kept twirling. It made Vince's eyes hurt. All he saw in his rearview mirror were those lights.

He hoped that it was a routine stop. There wasn't much traffic on the stretch of interstate at that time of night. He knew he had broken the speed limit, and he knew speeding was the stupidest thing he could have done. After what seemed like an hour, an officer sidled up to his window and rapped on it with his knuckle. Vince reached for the button to lower the window. Finding none, he grabbed the crank and rolled the window down manually. It felt odd doing something so mundane.

"Yes?" he asked.

"I need to see your driver's license and registration," the officer said.

Vince took his billfold from his pocket and slipped out his license. The officer took it. He shined his flashlight over it and then in Vince's face. His eyes throbbed from the glare. He turned away to open the glove box. It was empty. The armrest didn't have a console. He had no idea where Mary kept the registration.

"Registration, sir," the officer demanded.

"I can't seem to find it."

"Why do you think that is?"

"This is my wife's car, and I don't know where she keeps it."

"Your wife's car? Your license says you're from California, Mr. Green. The plates are from Florida. It just so happens I received a call about a stolen car with Florida plates in this model, make, and color from Jubilee a little ways down the interstate." The officer lowered the flashlight. "What do you think about that?"

"Ironic," Vince said.

"A little too ironic, don't you think?" the officer put the flashlight back through the loop on his belt. "Step out of the car, Mr. Green."

Vince waited for the officer to step back. He killed the engine and climbed out of the car. The officer turned him around to face the car. Hands started to pat him down after his own were placed on the roof. Fingers delved into his pockets, back and front. He felt the dread pat-down of his straddle and inseam.

"Mr. Green, place your hands behind your back," the officer said. "I'm arresting you for auto theft. You have the right to remain silent."

Vince let the officer handcuff him. The Miranda Rights faded into little more than a drone. He had no idea why he thought his luck would have kept up. Of course, he got caught. Stealing a car could get him prison time. Not any kind of prison time, but Southern prison time. He imagined swinging a blade, spaced out on a long dusty Alabama highway in the middle of the summer on some chain gang. Sweat already felt like it beaded on his forehead. They'd throw him in the hot box. Some big redneck with a Rebel flag tattoo would make him his bitch. He'd seen *Cool Hand Luke* too many times. The deputy would tell him what they had was a failure to communicate.

Instead, Vince fell over into the rear seat of the squad car after the cop escorted him there and shoved him in. The officer called for a wrecker. They waited for it. Vince sweated it out in the back seat. The officer sat on the hood of his car, smoking. A few diesels passed. One tooted its horn, and the officer waved at him. Finally the wrecker showed up. The car radio was set to a classic rock station—three-play nighttime, according to the DJ. Vince listened to "Tiny Dancer," "Philadelphia Freedom," and "Saturday Night's Alright (for Fighting)" while they hitched Mary's car to the wrecker. When the Eagles started harmonizing about a new kid in town, he wished he hadn't been the Johnny-come-lately.

The officer climbed into the front and switched off the radio.

"I got orders to take you back down to Jubilee. The wrecker's going to follow us."

"Is that normal? Are they going to put me out on the highway cutting weeds?" Vince rambled, too lost in his fantasy to know reality.

"What decade do you think this is?" the officer asked. "I'm carrying you back so they can house you in their jail. Marion County lockup is full. We don't have room for some other county's riffraff. It's bad enough the state has to put up with trash like you from California. Why can't y'all keep it in Compton?"

Vince realized that the patrol car had pulled onto the interstate and that he and the officer both held some incorrect stereotypes. Once they got back to Jubilee, Mary would bail him out and tell them it was all a misunderstanding.

The officer didn't take Vince to a police station. Instead they drove past the exit for Jubilee to one farther down the interstate. A message had come in over the radio advising the officer to take the perp—that's what he was being called—to a medical center. When he asked the officer why, all he got was silence.

The officer helped him out of the car and walked him through the sliding doors of the emergency room. A security guard met them. The officer took off the cuffs and handed Vince over to the guard.

"Are you Vincent Price Green?" the security guard, whose name badge called him Terrell, asked.

"Yes."

Several older patients in the waiting room stared at him when they heard his name. One old lady whispered to a man beside her and pointed to a TV mounted on the wall. As Terrell escorted him through the lobby, Vince glanced at the TV. His namesake, Vincent Price, stared back at him in Technicolor. He even recognized the movie, the Roger Corman classic *The Masque of the Red Death*. Vince was dragged through swinging metal doors into a long hallway.

"I can walk without being dragged," he said.

"I understand you were arrested for stealing a car," Terrell said.

"It was my ex-wife's, and I was borrowing it."

"*Sure.* I can't let a criminal loose in the hospital."

"Can you at least tell me where I'm being dragged off to?"

"The morgue."

"The morgue? Why?" Vince asked

"I don't know. I'm following orders."

They walked to an elevator that took them to the basement. The air felt cold down there. It smelled stale like most basements. They walked down a hallway lit with greenish fluorescent light until they came to a door marked morgue. Terrell opened it and pushed Vince inside.

A police officer stood as he entered the room. Mary slept, slumped over in a chair. A doctor in green scrubs wearing a surgical cap stayed seated behind a desk.

"This is Vincent Price Green," Terrell said.

"Good," the officer said. "We've been waiting for you. Miss, wake up. Your ex-husband is here."

Mary roused. When she recognized him, she jumped to her feet.

"They think they have Sara Beth's body in the morgue," she said, close to being hysterical. "We've been waiting for you so that we can identify it."

"We think a serial killer called the Peppermint Slasher got her," the officer said.

Although trepidation filled him up, Vince took a deep breath. He needed to stay calm in this situation. Mary always had a tendency to become overwrought. He doubted that had changed in her thirteen years of absence

"We've heard this story before," he said. "They thought they'd found my daughter in Memphis. The same guy was even accused of doing it."

"Let's have a look at her, doc," the officer said.

The doctor stood and unlocked the heavy metal door marked morgue. He held it opened as the officer walked inside. Vince took Mary by the arm and led her in as well. The door made a heavy clanging thud like a death knell when it closed. The morgue was small. Vince figured in a small hospital like this one, they didn't need room for more than about ten bodies. He counted fifteen drawers in the wall. Mary crossed her arms and rubbed her hands on them. The room was chilly. Small chill bumps rose on his exposed skin. It might have been the temperature or the idea that Sara Beth lay in one of those drawers.

"By the way, I'm Dr. Crawford, the pathologist," the doctor stopped at the drawer marked 7. "Understand that this body has been decomposing for some time, probably about two weeks, maybe more. It's going to be a bit shocking."

Vince nodded to the doctor. He couldn't speak. His breath caught in his throat. If it was his little girl in that drawer, he wasn't sure what he would do. He hoped to everything more powerful than himself that he wouldn't faint. It would do no one any good if he fell out.

The doctor, who Vince thought in the dimmer light of the morgue, looked like some ghoulish horror movie character, pulled out the drawer. A black body bag rested there. Vince's breathing steadied into long drawn breaths. He'd expected the body to be laid out naked to the world. Dr. Crawford stepped to the head of the bag. He pulled the zipper down two inches and stopped.

"Do you both want to look or only you?" he asked Vince.

"Mary?"

She shook her head and shrank backward. Vince looked at the cop and nodded his head toward her. The officer understood and stood beside Mary. Vince stepped up to the drawer, and he stood opposite the doctor. Another nod of this head signaled the doctor to continue pulling the zipper.

The bag fell back from the face. Although it was purple and blue and despite the film over the eyes and her hair matted with dirt and mud, Vince recognized Sara Beth. Even in that horrible condition, she appeared serene. His stomach did a somersault. He almost lost his supper on the floor. He nodded to Dr. Crawford, who zipped the bag back up.

"Is it?" Mary asked in a tiny voice that wasn't far from being a whimper.

Vince looked over his shoulder at her and nodded. She screamed. The sound wrenched so hard at Vince he thought he might explode. The sound of the drawer slamming shut took his attention away from her wail. Dr. Crawford took him by the elbow.

"There are some papers and formalities that need attending to," the doctor whispered to him. "We can do them now, or later."

"Now," Vince said. "I've got myself steeled hard right now. Later on, I doubt I'll be this sturdy."

He knew that he would be in no condition later. If the formalities took too long, he might lose the ability to handle things in the middle of the paperwork. They all walked back to the office. The dreariness of it was a welcomed change of scenery from the oppressive morgue.

Chapter Thirty-two

Once things settled down at the inn, the Wasp went for a moonlit walk. It had been a long time since he'd walked in the night without the intention of killing. Tonight there were more pressing matters than the gnawing need to commit murder. Although he had the money to pay off the Silver Lady's mortgage bill and her other debts, it would be only a temporary fix. She needed something more permanent, and he needed her to need him. All he wanted in return was her love. The Wasp didn't need sexual love and rarely craved it. The Silver Lady needed to love him like the grandmother she was.

The town lay asleep before him. No cars moved down the streets. Not a single light illuminated the windows of the houses he passed. He was like the great white shark cruising through the dark ocean depths. Any of the people sleeping behind those doors could be his victim, but for tonight, everyone was safe.

He stopped walking when he came to the Jaycee fairgrounds on the other side of downtown. Two metal gates blocked the paved driveway into the flat open space. Only a cable ran from those gates to poles marking the corners. The dark structure of a Ferris wheel loomed over the place. It went to the sky. The skeletal silhouette was awe-inspiring.

The Wasp always liked the fair. It was easy to find victims and even easier to escape unnoticed. Anytime a carnival came around, the police profiled carnies as perpetrators of crimes more than anyone else during that time. The Wasp felt that they were nasty people who lived in a constant state of depravity, even worse than the addicts he killed on a consistent basis.

He stepped over the cable and entered the sleeping carnival. As he walked across the fairgrounds, he found that all the rides were set up and ready. Even the game tents lined the midway. As he walked down the quiet path, his imagination filled with the sounds of the carnival. The lights of the rides dazzled in his mind's eye. The smells of the treats flourished in his nose. The thing he noticed most was the permeating scent of peppermint. Usually the odor of the food had an undertone of vomit expelled from riders on the Tilt-A-Whirl or the Scrambler. When he stopped to give the place a good looking at, the Wasp found that he stood by a tent with a name placard that read "Bellflower's Confections" over the top of the booth.

The Silver Lady would peddle her wares there in a night or so. All her hopes for the future would hang on the sales, if she could make them. Probably one of those disgusting carnies would swindle her out of her money. Although he knew she could kill without much remorse, the Wasp found the Silver Lady a bit naïve when it came to the ways of the real world.

"Can I help you," a raspy voice asked from the darkness.

The Wasp smelled the sweet aroma of a cheap cigar. He turned to find a long-haired man with a gray beard that touched his chest. A rubber band held the braid in his beard. In the moonlight, the Wasp could see the nastiness of the man's T-shirt and the grease stains on his jeans. He held a baseball bat in one hand. Brass knuckles covered the other. The guy would have intimidated anyone else but the Wasp.

"Just looking," the Wasp said.

"We ain't opened yet," the man said. "I suggest you get on down the road."

"I was checking on my booth." The Wasp wished he'd brought his trusty knife with him.

"Are you Bellflower?" the carnie asked.

"Maybe."

"I thought she was an old broad."

"I'm her grandson." The Wasp let a Southern accent color his voice enough to be noticed. "She said I needed to check to make sure everything was in order."

"At 4:30 in the morning?"

"I was on my way to work. I thought I'd stop by."

"How come your accent changed?"

"It did no such of a thing," the Wasp said.

"I heard it. When I first started talking to you, it was a Yankee accent. Now it ain't."

"When was the last time you washed out that shirt, or come to that, your ears?"

The carnie eyed him. The Wasp felt it. Spending as much time as he had in the dark, doing things that didn't need to be seen, gave him an extra sense for maneuvering in low light. Now he needed to maneuver out of there.

"You've seen. Now get to moving," the carnie said, not amused by being called dirty and dumb.

"My thoughts exactly."

The Wasp gave the carnie a slight bow and moved away. He walked at a good pace but not so much as to make the guy with a bat think he was running scared. In fact, he wasn't. The Wasp could have handled that guy even without his knife. Only the Silver Lady needed him. She especially needed to hear his plan for making the money to not only save her house, but also to put her up in lavender for the rest of her days. Little did that slimy carnie know, but he'd helped him see the next steps with perfect clarity.

He thought again about how the fair was the perfect place to find a victim and escape without being noticed. The Wasp held keeping a low profile as a commandment, along with limiting the DNA evidence—and never let anyone get a good look at you. His primary commandment was never do anything to get caught. That rule was paramount. Doing anything to that despicable carnie would violate the primary edict, and the Wasp had already violated enough of his commandments when he met the Silver Lady. She had a way of making him shatter his stone tablets into powder. She was his idol, a silver calf to be worshipped.

Chapter Thirty-three

Camilla checked the candies in her display cases. It had been several days since she'd opened the store. Some of the merchandise would have gone stale. Graham had come into her room not long after dawn and told her that she had to open the store today. He insisted on coming to work with her. She knew it was futile to argue with him or even open the shop doors. No one wanted to buy candy from a store where a decomposing murder victim had been found. Fortunately, the police didn't have any part of the store shut off except out back, and she didn't need that space. Camilla needed to go to the store anyway. The shop might never make another dime, but the apple tent at the fair would. She needed to get a large portion of the candy apples finished. If people happened to come in for some other kind of confection, Graham could wait on them so she could focus on the real money-makers.

"I'll man the front so you can start making those candied apples for the fair," Graham said, walking from the kitchen tying on an apron.

"Don't expect much business. I hope you have a book to read or otherwise you're going to get bored," she said.

"You'll see. I know what I'm talking about."

Camilla shrugged and headed to the back. A crate of apples rested on the counter. She'd come in after Lily's death long enough to take the delivery of fruit. They looked good, nice and red. The perfect apples to candy. The Granny Smiths didn't look too bad either. She used them as a platform for her patented golden caramel. It was so sweet and decadent that the tartness of the green apples helped to cut the cloying sweetness.

She heard Graham talking up front. He frightened her when he responded to the voices in his head. How could a sane person do the heinous things he had done? As she took out a red apple from the crate and shoved a wooden skewer into it, she realized that she'd never heard voices and she had done some heinous things as much as he had. But it was different. She never mutilated people. Her job was to keep her family together, despite all obstacles. Someone answered Graham back. Camilla realized that either she too was crazy, or there was a customer up front. Without thinking, she walked to the doorway so she could peek into the showroom.

Mrs. Spence stood at the counter. She pointed into the display case at the peanut brittle that Camilla knew was getting to the point that it would be a dicey choice for a confection. Graham took one of her little pink and black striped boxes and started to fill it up with the treat.

"My sons Ricky and Jimmy love this stuff. I usually make my own, but I don't have the time. I know that Camilla's is extra tasty," Mrs. Spence said to Graham.

"I like it a lot," Graham said with put-on Southern charm oozing in every word.

"I've never seen you in here before," she said.

He folded the lid over the top of the box. "You ought to come in more often."

Mrs. Spence smiled and giggled like a girl who was being flirted with. "If I'd known you were in here, I would have." She looked past him to Camilla. "You should've told us you had such a handsome man working in here."

"He's new," Camilla said. "I've got some cashew brittle over there. You might want to see if Ricky and Jimmy like it."

Mrs. Spence looked where she pointed. Her eyes lit up. "I'll take some of it, too." She paused and bit her lip as if she had something to say that embarrassed her. "You wouldn't happened to have any peppermint would you?"

Camilla shook her head. "No, ma'am. I haven't made any of that in a while."

"Too bad. I was in the mood for some homemade peppermint. I guess the brittle will do."

Graham packed her up a box of the cashew brittle. He rang up her purchase, took her money, got a tip that he shoved into his pocket, and wished her a good day. As soon as Mrs. Spence walked out, Mrs. Bartlett walked in.

"Can I help you?" Graham asked.

"When did you get him?" Bartlett asked.

"He's helping me out until after the fair," Camilla said. "So that I can focus on getting apples ready. Lily used to help me, but..."

"I'm glad you're still doing the fair apples. The mayor and I wondered if you would after everything that has happened." She looked in the cases and appeared disappointed. "No peppermints?"

"I've not made them in a while."

Bartlett sighed. "I guess I'll take some fudge then, a small box."

Graham assisted her, and she left. Camilla started back into the kitchen to work. He walked in as she was shoving the skewers into the apples.

"Why don't you let me do this?" he asked.

"I can handle it."

"I think you should make up some peppermint-flavored items," Graham said.

"Why?"

"Morbid fascination," he said. "You've had two customers who haven't been in here for a while. They both wanted peppermint. The news has gotten out about the body, or more likely what was found in the body. The gruesome and grotesque interest people. A girl was buried in the back of the store with a peppermint inside her. They want the same candy associated with the notorious location. A memento of death, like how people in the old days would cut pieces of cloth from the clothes of the executed."

"You made that up," she said.

"No, when they executed royalty—back when chopping off heads was the going thing—peasants and others would soak rags in the blood. Peppermint is this town's version of that."

"That's sick." She felt a little nauseous.

"Maybe, but you can sell bags of homemade peppermints for as much as you want. I bet they'll sell like hotcakes at the fair. Maybe you should think about making a peppermint apple."

"Peppermint and apples don't mix. Making peppermint-flavored treats feels dirty, like profiting from the poor girl's death."

Graham stabbed a skewer into a plump apple. A look of impish glee crossed his lips. "You were going to, anyway. Remember the necklace?"

He was right. There was no reason to refuse when she was so desperate for money. She hoped that the people of the community didn't look down on her for it, though.

Someone tapped on the counter. Graham impaled another apple. She couldn't help but notice his knack for stabbing. It took so little effort. It terrified her. He smiled and headed back to the front of the store.

"Yes, ma'am?" he asked.

"Does Miss Bellflower have any peppermint candy?" the customer asked.

"We sold out," Graham said with his newfound charming voice. "She's starting another batch. Come back in a few hours or so, and we'll have a ton of it."

"I will."

He looked back at Camilla as she started to measure out the sugar to make the candies. A wicked smile of a deviant grandchild—one who got caught with his hand in the cookie jar—curled on his lips.

***

One of the county deputies dropped Vince off back at the Bellflower Inn. After ten hours of questioning, he felt completely drained. When Vince stepped into the parlor, the old-lady smell of the place hit him hard in the face, stronger than he'd ever noticed in the past. The door slammed behind him. He didn't mean for it to, but it did.

Mary came out of the kitchen, wiping her hands on an apron that was too frilly and made her look like some kind of June

163

Cleaver wannabe. She couldn't be farther from that wholesome character unless the zombie apocalypse had claimed June Cleaver.

"Are you just getting back from the sheriff's department?" she asked.

"No, I thought that I'd go fishing after finding out my daughter had been murdered by some vicious psychopath and enduring hours of questioning. They weren't biting, so I came home." He smiled a sarcastic smile. "Of course, I've been at the sheriff's. You turned me in for auto theft."

"You did take my car in the middle of the night without asking," Mary said, not giving in to his indignation.

"I was going to bring it back."

She shook her head. "No you weren't. You were heading to California, leaving me here with the Golden Girls."

"I still didn't deserve being grilled about whether I killed my own daughter. They actually seriously considered me a suspect."

"I'm sorry about that, but you did steal a car, and your story sounds a little strange."

"A little strange? Every word is true, and you know that. Instead of coming to my defense, you let me get raked over the hot coals."

"I'm sorry. Why don't you have something to eat?"

"I'm going to bed and try to sleep. Maybe I will later."

He left Mary standing there and mounted the stairs. His eyes barely stayed opened. He couldn't remember the last time he'd been so exhausted, the kind of fatigue that only the Old Testament character of Job might have endured.

Vince opened the door to his room and stepped inside. He moved on autopilot. His clothes came off, and he flopped onto the bed, not bothering to draw the covers over himself. A scent from the pillows filled his nostrils. It wasn't his smell.

He sat up and opened his eyes. The pillow case was yellow. The room the Bellflowers had let to him was decorated in blue, including all the bed clothes. He rolled over and stared around. The wallpaper bore little yellow daisies on it. A small round table with a yellow doily served as the night stand. A chest of drawers topped with a mirror sat against the wall. The curtains were yellow lace. A pair of motorcycle boots sat under a straight-back chair with a pair of blue jeans slung over it. He'd wandered into Graham's room.

Vince stood up and walked to the door gathering his clothes as he did. As he passed the boots, he glanced down at them. They looked expensive for a guy who seemed to be hoboing around the country on his bike. In the left one, something shiny caught his attention. He reached down and took it out. A knife with a serrated edge as long as the boot glimmered in the light. It looked fierce. A tool meant more for filleting than whittling at a Boy Scout jamboree.

He gave the room another glance. A black billfold made for the front pocket lay on the chest of drawers. Vince dropped the knife back into the boot and took up the wallet. He found several different driver's licenses in it. One was from Oregon with Graham's picture, but his name was Thomas Tillis. A Washington State license named him Omar Cayenne. The only one that identified him as Graham Chapman was from Nevada. Vince found licenses with aliases from California, Arizona, New Mexico and Idaho. The guy calling himself Graham Chapman got around.

The exhaustion that pulled at him so strongly a moment before evaporated. Vince started going through the drawers. He found a roll of money in a rubber band under three pairs of black Fruit of Loom boxer briefs. In another drawer, which held some black socks, he found a half empty bag of peppermint candy.

"He's the killer," Vince whispered. "Jesus Christ, he ate dinner with us. Listened to me talk about my daughter and told me about meeting her. The whole time he stayed as cool as an ocean breeze."

He put the stuff back. Graham didn't know that he knew. That was his advantage. Vince would call the cops and tell them he'd found the guy. The problem was he had no real evidence. Graham carried a boot knife. A lot of bikers did. He had money and some fake IDs. He was probably some small-time pool hustler. The flight of fancy faded away, and the fatigue set in again. Vince knew he was being silly. His tired mind had led him down the path of paranoia. He wanted so much to discover who had killed his daughter that he might even be able to find a reason to think old Camilla had done it. A laugh escaped him.

Vince left Graham's room and entered his own. As soon as he crashed onto his blue-clothed bed, he fell asleep. Nightmares started almost as soon as he'd dozed off.

Chapter Thirty-four

A couple with their little girl left the shop. The daddy looked like a lawyer, wearing a suit the Wasp thought looked too expensive for the town. His wife wore a large diamond on her finger. They'd bought the same thing as everyone else who'd come through the store that day had—peppermint candies.

The Silver Lady had made several different peppermint treats. Only a few squares of peppermint fudge remained. She came from the back carrying a small box of candied apples. Somehow during the rush of the day, she'd been able to make those as well. The Wasp tried to learn how to do it so he could help her, but the customers had kept him busy selling the peppermints.

"Are those for the fair tonight?" he asked. "I think you'll need more."

"I'm taking these back to the house. These are for our dessert this evening."

"Aren't we going to the fair," he said, counting the money from the register. "We made a lot of money today. You could have charged double for those candies."

"That would be gouging," she said. "It wouldn't be neighborly of me."

"I guess it wouldn't, but your neighbors coming by to gawk at the murder shop isn't too neighborly either. Especially considering your sister recently passed away here too."

The Silver Lady thought about this before telling him he was right. The Wasp finished putting the money into a deposit envelope, and they left. The night trended warm. The humidity felt low, however. It would be a good night to set up at the fair. He almost looked forward to it. He worked over his plan in his head. It would be easy to accomplish at the fair given the right amount of time. Unfortunately, there were several factors that needed to play into his hands. Complicated plans oftentimes fell apart, but the Wasp liked solving problems. It always gave him a sense of accomplishment. If that lawyer from earlier in the day had friends who liked the fair, he and the Silver Lady would be rolling in the dough before the carnival rode out of town.

"What time do we have to be at the fair?" he asked.

"We're not going tonight," the Silver Lady opened the door to her car.

"Why not? It is the opening night, isn't it?"

"Yeah, but we're not invited tonight."

"I thought you said they loved your apples." The Wasp sat in the passenger seat.

The Silver Lady handed him the box of apples and fastened her seat belt. He fumbled to secure his. On the way to the shop that morning, her driving proved that some things could still shake his steely nerves. She pulled the car onto the empty street. They sped too fast to the corner, where he nearly slammed into the dash when the Silver Lady hit the brakes.

"They do love my apples," she finally said. "Tonight isn't opened to the general public. It's for the special people. Only the game booths are opened. I think the fair concession stand is as well."

"You mean the local yokel celebs don't want you to sell your apples to them?"

She looked at him, ignoring the road. The Wasp tried hard to not show how uncomfortable her driving made him, unwilling to reveal a weakness for her to exploit. Although he felt like they had grown close quickly, he never needed a potential enemy to know of any chink in his armor.

"Special doesn't mean that kind of people. I mean *touched*," she said.

"Touched? Like kids that have been molested?" He knew that question sounded stupid, but he didn't know what she meant.

"Special people like retarded people. Mongoloids and such," she said.

That word made the Wasp laugh out loud. He'd not heard it in a long time. It amazed him how nonchalantly the Silver Lady said *mongoloid*. He figured she would have had more class than that.

"I know that they don't call them that anymore," she said, defensively, "but I can't remember what it's called."

"Down syndrome."

"That's it. The first night of the spring fair is always opened for the special people. The community pays for it. The carnival people have only one stipulation, no outside vendors. They give the community a good discount so they want to make as much money as possible. We'll set up tomorrow night."

"I look forward to it."

The Silver Lady stopped in front of her house and climbed out of the car, taking the box from him. He got out after her. The sun gave enough light for them to see onto the porch. Only a lamp lit the parlor. The Wasp broke off from the Silver Lady and headed up to his room. He wanted to check on things and then head to the bathroom to wash up. His arms and face felt sticky. A lot of sugar had been melted around him and gave him a sweet sheen.

He noticed things were out of sorts as soon as he walked into his room. Someone had rifled through his things. He couldn't put his finger on what gave him that impression, but it was fact. Just like the three bears, someone had been sleeping in his bed. The indention of a body messed up the duvet cover. The drawers had been opened. His boots had been disturbed as well. The place didn't look any cleaner, so he doubted it had been Tunie freshening up the accommodations. Either Vince or his ex-wife had been here. He'd bet real money they were looking for evidence of who he was. The sense of paranoia made him antsy.

The Wasp knew paranoia. He suffered from occasional bouts of it when he felt the heat getting close. There was no way that Vince or his ex-wife could know that he was the Peppermint Slasher. It bothered him that he hadn't locked his door. He'd given the rubes too little credit. Vince was from Cali. The Wasp should have known he'd be sneaky.

When he heard a tap on the door, the Wasp wheeled around

ready to attack. The door cracked opened enough for Vince to slip his head inside.

"Can I come in?" he asked.

The Wasp smiled. It would be much easier to take care of him behind the closed door. He could always say that Vince attacked him after ranting crazy accusations. If he had to kill the man, it would be self-defense. A Yankee with a record for stealing cars wouldn't be held in high regard by the local boys.

"That's fine," the Wasp said.

Vince came in and closed the door. He looked rough. The Wasp didn't usually take notice of men's appearance, but the bags under Vince's eyes were so dark he looked as if he'd been in a boxing match. His hair stood up everywhere. The whiskers on his face had passed the five o'clock shadow twelve hours before.

"The murdered girl was Sara Beth," Vince said, almost emotionless.

The Wasp found Vince's lack of emotion strange. He chalked it up to his being so exhausted.

"I'm sorry to hear that."

"They kept me at the jail for a while, asking me all kinds of questions. They thought I did it. Why would I kill my own daughter? Worse than that, why would I act like some sociopath and shove a peppermint up her ass?"

The Wasp gritted his teeth. He didn't like being called a sociopath. When a newscaster would say that, he usually busted the TV. But it wasn't going to provoke him to that kind of reaction this time. He could hold it together in tight little knots in his stomach for as long as it took.

"Cops are strange."

"I wanted to tell you. I guess that girl you saw wasn't her. They said she'd been dead for a while."

"Again I'm sorry. By the way, someone has been in here today."

"It was me. I wandered in thinking it was my room. I didn't touch anything," Vince said.

"Yes, you did."

The Wasp pointed at the bed, next to the chest of drawers, and finally to the boots. Vince followed his finger. His face showed that he'd been caught in a lie. There was only one thing that the Wasp hated more than being called a sociopath, and that was being lied to, especially by someone like Vince.

"I laid down on your bed. When I realized I was in the wrong room, I started out. I noticed the knife in your boot so I looked at. Then I was all paranoid so I looked in your drawers." Vince chuckled. "For a moment I thought you were the Peppermint Slasher."

The Wasp chuckled back. "Why is that?"

"The peppermint candies in your drawer."

"They keep my mouth moist while I ride my bike. Sometimes its cinnamon discs, sometimes butterscotch. I prefer lemon drops, but the last gas station I stopped at only had peppermint," he said, hoping that he sound offended but not defensive.

"I was being paranoid. The notion passed as quickly as I had it. You're too clean cut to be that much of a kook. I was past the point of exhaustion."

The Wasp tightened his jaw. With taut lips, he said, "I'm hungry. I need to wash up."

Vince left without saying another word. The Wasp stood in his room, staring into the hall. His *friend* had become a serious liability. He would have to take care of him. In a way that was good, because the blood lust had built up so high that he wouldn't be able to keep it under control much longer. When it got too strong, he made stupid mistakes.

The Wasp stepped to the bathroom, washed his hands, and went down to dinner. The whole while he plotted how to deal with Vincent Price Green. If he could play it right, everything would fall into place so the Silver Lady got her money, too. He would get away with another murder, and Vince would bite the big one for it. The Wasp almost laughed but caught himself. No need to tip his hand to the junior sleuth, Hardy Boy wannabe who had been standing in his room.

Chapter Thirty-five

After another busy day of selling peppermint treats to macabre townspeople, Camilla breathed in the fair. The air smelled like fried food, mud and human mass. The lights flashed. Music from every imaginable genre rose in a cacophony of sound that if she'd heard it on the street, it would have made her head hurt. At the fair, none of that mattered. It was the sound of money and hope. For the first time since her dear sister Lily died, Camilla felt happy and lighthearted.

The booth looked as it always did. The town had stored her tent in one of its supply sheds with the tents they used for the livestock show and arts-and-crafts contests. Red and white checkered gingham table clothes covered the rustic counters she'd been using for at least twenty years. Graham helped her spread the apples on them. Cellophane wrapped around each apple. In the old days, she tied little festive bows around the top to keep the plastic wrap closed. Arthritis ended that tradition a long time ago.

"I love the fair," she said to no one in particular.

"What was that?" Graham unloaded a box of caramel Granny Smiths.

Camilla refocused on the present, emerging from her floaty daydream. "Nothing. I was thinking about how much I love the fair."

"I don't care too much for them," he said. "These carnies are shady folks."

She looked over at him. He had a lot of room calling other people shady. Her new grandson's main hobby was cutting up girls and sticking peppermints inside them. The patrons who'd bought peppermint-flavored treats from him over the last two days would have gotten a real kick out of that. It seemed strange to her that he should have some kind of moral code that found carnival folk distasteful.

"I figured you would love them," she spread out a cloth, over which she would pass treats to the customers. "Easy pickings."

Graham gave her a look of displeasure. "I have standards."

His words seemed harsh. Again the idea that someone so obviously psychopathic had standards floored her. Camilla didn't know much about serial killers beyond the true crime books she liked to read. She never thought she'd meet one until he showed up like something from a nightmare, where everything seems both real and surreal at the same time. Ever since, the idea kept her awake some nights. It mostly mingled in with her longing to see her sister again. Her whole life had been devoted to keeping the sisters together.

Lily's husband was the first to try to keep them apart. Because he was by no means the definition of healthy even by the standards of the 1950s, it surprised no one when he dropped dead of an apparent heart attack. The poison used back then took a while to work. He'd been complaining to Lily of pains and feeling unwell, but he never did anything about it. That was Camilla's first dealings with murder. If she had realized the extent it would play in her life, she would have done something about it way back then. Tunie's serious beau was the second, although her younger sister had no idea he was dead. Camilla got good at faking people's handwriting. The letter to Tunie convinced her that he'd decided to leave town forever. Her sister was always naive and bought it. After that, it was a string of hobos and lodgers that had no place to be and no one to look for them. The whole time she'd cleaned up the messes to keep Tunie from realizing what she'd done, and to keep Lily in a happy place of ignorance concerning how far gone their baby sister's mental state had become.

The small bell on the counter dinged. Camilla turned and saw a family she recognized from her store. The children were big-eyed. The parents looked almost the same.

"Candy apples?" she asked.

The two kids nodded their heads. The mother and father did the same. She grabbed four of the candy-coated treats. Her apples would not keep the doctor away. If anyone with bad teeth got a hold of one, it would definitely bring about a visit to the dentist.

They paid her and walked away.

"Our first sale?" Graham said, stepping up the counter.

"Hopefully one of many more." Camilla shoved the money into the pocket of her apron.

"You know that even if you sell every one of these apples at twice what you're asking, you won't make the money you need, right?" Graham asked.

"I'll make enough."

"Enough to get right back into the same situation in a matter of weeks," Graham paused. He sold two apples to a couple. When they walked out of earshot he continued. "You're getting too old to keep up the kill-lonely-guests game."

Camilla turned on him. How dare he talk like that right in the open? It was as if he wanted them to get caught. She'd taken a great risk not turning him in, and now he had her in a tight spot. It was like making a deal with the devil. No one would believe that Tunie had done it all.

"You shouldn't talk about that kind of stuff here," she said.

"The music's too loud, and people are too excited to care," he said.

Timothy O'Hare, his wife, and little girl stepped up to the counter. Camilla recognized him from his law firm ads in the newspaper and their visit to the shop yesterday. Before she could serve them, Graham stepped forward.

"What can I get y'all?" he asked, faking a Southern accent.

"Two candy apples and one caramel," the father said, holding out the money.

Graham took the cash and gave the man change. Then he grabbed the order and passed it off to them.

"Thank you," Camilla said.

"You know that this lady kills people with poisoned candy," Graham said out of the blue. "Then she blames it on her crazy sister."

Camilla's chin stiffened. The muscles in her chest tightened. She thought she might swallow her tongue. Timothy laughed as did his wife. Even the little girl chuckled. The customers shook their heads and walked away.

"No one cares," he said. "At the fair, they think everything is a joke."

Camilla wheeled around on him. She pressed her finger into his chest.

"Don't you ever do that again," she said. "Keep your mouth shut, and when this fair is done, I want you gone."

Graham grabbed her wrist and squeezed hard enough to cause her to flinch. His fingers crushed into her arthritic joints, and his smile never wavered. Nothing lived behind his eyes except pure, inexhaustible evil.

"I'm not going anywhere. We're a team now."

"You will, and we're not a team."

"If I don't leave, what are you going to do, sic Tunie on me?" he said. "According to you, she only kills in what psychiatrists call a fugue state. Those aren't on command."

"I'll do something."

"It won't help," Graham said.

"Why not?"

"Vince has notions."

"What kind of notions?" Camilla tried to pull away from him, but he wouldn't let her.

"The kind that could get us caught. He snooped in my room and found things."

"And?"

"If I go down, I'm dragging you with me, old woman. Don't get me wrong. I love you like I would my own grandmother, maybe more, but I'd slit my own granny's throat if I thought I was going down."

He let go. Camilla rubbed her wrist. For the first time, Graham outright scared her. She needed to come up with some way to get rid of him. She'd never planned something so devious, but she had no choice.

"Why don't you take care of him?" she asked. "You seem skilled at getting rid of people."

"I've already thought about that," Graham said. "First things first. I'm going to earn us all the money you need."

He took one of the caramel apples and left the tent. Camilla watched him disappear into the swell of bodies on the midway, wishing she could call the police and rid herself of the albatross around her neck. They were Siamese twins of crime. If one failed to thrive, they were both goners. She didn't know how she'd let herself get in that position.

So many years of being stealthy undone by some drifter. In the back of her mind, she felt the loneliness she'd always feared the most. Tunie was still around—but for how long? She slipped more and more everyday into her own little world of adolescent memories. Camilla felt trapped in a gilded cage by Graham. She was a canary singing to an empty room. The loneliness stabbed at her vital organs like no knife Graham could ever wield. She wanted to cry and to scream at the same time, but she could do neither.

Camilla took a customer's money and gave her an apple. It was an automatic function. Something that had to be done whether she was lonely or not. Selling those apples might be the only thing that could save her from her worst nightmare—slowly evolving from being completely alone to being alone with Graham Chapman.

Chapter Thirty-six

The flashing lights and festive sounds of the fair did little to tamp down the Wasp's feelings. For some reason, the Silver Lady acted far different than he had expected. They were like family, linked by their common bond of murder. The problem was she thought she was better than him.

Somehow she'd gotten it into her head that what she did was justified, and what he did was plain, senseless, psychopathic killing. The Silver Lady thought because she had been doing her thing for decades longer that she was smarter. But for all her cleverness, she was now caught by the short hairs and needed to be bailed out. Her thin stories about her crazy sister wouldn't hold up to any kind of scrutiny. He was the only one with the ability and love to help her. Now she had to depend on some roughneck slasher, and it bothered her.

It bothered him that she was not more receptive. He had to prove his worth to her, and he would do that beyond her wildest dreams. The plan changed on the wing. He didn't have time for the complicated one. Simplicity always worked better anyway.

He stepped from behind the line of booths onto the midway. Lots of people milled around. The game tents were crowded with lines of people. Screams echoed out as some strange twirling ride gave the patrons a thrill that can only be experienced at the fair. The Wasp wore his blinders. All this became unseen peripheral information. His sights were set on the prize, and that wasn't some cheap stuffed Scooby Doo or Sponge Bob Square Pants. He began to troll the crowd. As he vanished amongst them, his persona changed.

As he shifted through the current of bodies, his belly pooched out, pulling the fabric of his T-shirt tight around it. His shoulders slumped like a man who had been worked too hard or lacked all self-esteem. He felt his jaw go slack. This, he knew, would give him the appearance of idiocy. Finally, he let his eyes droop.

Passing past the fun house with its funny mirrors on the side, the Wasp caught a glimpse of himself. He could walk up to the Silver Lady's booth right now, and she wouldn't recognize him. No one would. The Wasp looked like some slow-witted yokel. He needed one more thing to sell the image. With a quick flourish of his hand, his hair stood up at angles that gave it an uncombed appearance. He could have gotten into the *special people's* night yesterday without question.

The test of his new persona was about to come. The police officers he'd encountered the night he killed Lily Bellflower stood near the central kiosk. He strode past them, making sure to bump into Officer Jones.

"Excuse me," he slurred his words while adding a thick Southern accent.

"Watch where you're going," Jones said not looking at him.

Officer Smith nudged his partner. Jones looked at the Wasp. His face softened from the hard look of annoyance to one of piteous sympathy.

"I'm sorry," the Wasp said again, now bucking his teeth out for added effect.

"No problem," Jones said. "Are you here by yourself?"

The Wasp shook his head. "We had such a good time last night that my group home came back."

"That's good. Enjoy yourself and don't get lost. Don't eat too many of those apples. They'll give you a tummy ache."

The Wasp nodded and drifted off, staring at the flashing neon like a simpleton might do. His new persona was complete. He could get away with anything, and these people would be looking for a slow-witted man from one of the local group homes as the suspect. All he needed now was the prize.

He spotted a little girl he recognized from the apple booth. She had been with a wealthy family. Now she stood alone near the Tilt-a-Whirl, looking lost. No one else noticed her. He walked over near her, still looking around as if he was taking in all the wonderment. His arm knocked into her. His apple hit the ground He looked down to apologize. She was looking up at him. Tears brimmed her eyes. He knew they weren't a result of the impact, but because the little girl was lost and afraid. Those were the kind of tears he'd seen many times.

"I'm sorry," he said. "I didn't hurt you, did I?"

"No." Her voice barely held back the sobs. "I can't find my parents."

"You're lost?"

"Uh huh. I stopped to watch this ride, and when I turned to tell them I wanted to go on it, they were gone."

"Oh, no. I saw some policemen back over there. Come with me, and I'll take you to them."

"I'm not supposed to go with strangers," she said.

"They're right over there," the Wasp made himself sound much more innocent.

The little girl softened. "You dropped your apple."

"I'll get another one. Come on."

She held out her small hand to him. He took it with a gentle simpleton's touch. The girl gave him all her trust. It always made his job a lot easier.

"I'm Alice. What's your name?" she asked.

"Vince. Vince Green." The Wasp said the name louder than he had been talking, hoping that if some passerby took notice, they might remember the name.

She nodded, and he led her toward the kiosk. Then he looked to the side where two booths separated to the back area as if he'd spotted something. He pointed.

"There they go," he said. "There go the policemen."

With a quick motion, he pulled her that way, not giving her time to think or to jerk away. When they were behind the booths, his hand went over her mouth. She struggled and bit his fingers, but her teeth didn't break the skin. Pain never bothered him. Before she could do anything else, they were over the back fence and headed into a wooded area beyond the fairground. The deep shadows of the night hid them only yards from the excitement of the carnival. Now all he had to do was get her back to the Bellflower Inn without being seen. The shed behind the place was the perfect place to store the little brat. The Wasp was certain it contained lots of secrets. He bet that the Silver Lady kept some skeletons buried there, so he assumed it would be the most secure location.

Chapter Thirty-seven

Vince's drive to the pizzeria was uneventful. He was glad of that. After his last excursion in Mary's car, he worried about driving it anywhere even with her permission. The small-town police he'd dealt with so far would love to bust him again. Vince needed to get out of town as soon as possible. Of course, money was the problem. He had to wait until the first of the month so he could ship Sara Beth's body back to California for a proper burial. There was no way he'd leave her in Alabama, a place she'd only visited once and that was to die.

He parked behind Graham's motorcycle. The car's headlights illuminated the back of it.

Graham owned a fine bike, and Vince took a moment to admire it. He wished he had one like it. Maybe when he returned home and landed another job, he'd buy one. It had been a long time since he'd treated himself to more than a pepperoni pizza. Something caught his eye as he climbed out of the car. The headlights clicked off. He put them back on high beams. A Mississippi license plate hung on the back of the bike. It didn't make sense, because Graham said he'd come from California, riding it the whole way. The motorcycle clearly had Mississippi tags. He couldn't deny that fact.

Vince turned off the lights and grabbed the pizza. He hurried into the house. Mary met him almost as soon as he walked inside. She took the box from him.

"What took you so long?" she asked. "Miss Tunie and I are starving."

"I was admiring Graham's bike," he said.

"You can do that later. Come on and eat."

"Is he here?"

"Graham? No, he's still at the fair with Camilla," Mary said.

"You two go ahead and eat. I've got something I want to do. I may need to borrow the car again. Please, don't call the police."

Vince walked back outside.

He opened the car and turned the headlights back on. He walked over to the bike and opened one of the saddlebags. Rifling around in it, he found little more than some plastic bags and a rain suit. The other saddlebag had a hard plastic box in it. Vince opened it and found paperwork sealed in a quart-size freezer bag. The registration for the bike was from Hinds County, Mississippi. According to the document, the bike's title belonged to a man named Leroy Anderson Washington III. A bill of sale was also in the box. It belonged to Leroy Anderson Washington III. Three plastic cards lay under the paperwork. The first was a debit card for Leroy. The second was a Discover credit card. The third was a Mississippi driver's license. Its photograph was faded, and in the shadow he cast over the bike, Vince couldn't make out much about it. He took the cards back to the car. In the interior car light, he saw the face of a black man, probably well in his fifties, pictured on the license. The birth date confirmed the age. The name was Leroy Anderson Washington III.

"He stole the bike," Vince said out loud.

Without thinking, he tossed the cards on the passenger seat and started the car. He headed toward the fairgrounds. Something wasn't right about Graham. The bike registration and odd conglomeration of IDs he'd found in Graham's room didn't add up to any good sum. Graham was hiding something from them all. Vince knew that whatever the secret was, it wasn't good. He was certain that the man calling himself Graham Chapman was dangerous. Vince now felt like he shouldn't have dismissed the possibility of Graham being a killer. He'd been charming enough to pull the wool over Vince's eyes. From watching TV programs and reading about psychopaths, he knew they could be chameleons. The police needed to know.

They wouldn't believe him, though. He was certain of that. They'd spent too much time trying to make him Sara Beth's killer. They still had him pegged as a prime suspect. If he told them some story about Graham, the police would dismiss it as him trying to clear his name.

Vince had to find Graham and confront him, alone. It was the only way to learn the truth.

A part of him hoped Graham was the Peppermint Slasher. Vince would take sweet pleasure in getting rid of the man who took his daughter away from him. Even if he spent the rest of his life in jail—or died trying—he would know that he'd done something to try to right the wrong that had been done to Sara Beth.

***

Customers surrounded the candy apple tent. Camilla could barely keep up with the demand. She hadn't expected Graham to bail on her. Now, she didn't know what else to expect. He was a bit of a crazy. Officer Jones stood next in line. He handed her his money.

"Caramel," Jones said.

"One caramel." She stretched to grab one of the green apples smothered in the creamy golden confection. Her joints popped from the strain. The arthritis wasn't used to giving up that much stretch.

"Working alone? I'd thought you'd have help. Doesn't Tunie usually lend you a hand?" Jones asked.

"Normally, but she hasn't been quite right since Lily died. Our boarder, Graham Chapman, came with me. He's been learning the candy-making trade for the last few days." She made his change.

"Where is he, on a break?"

"No, he blew out on me."

Jones took the apple. "Did you say Graham Chapman?"

"Yeah," Camilla moved on to another customer and started filling their order.

"I met him the other night. The night you found your sister. He said that he worked with the carnival," Jones said.

"You must be mistaken. He's from California, riding across country after his mother's death," she lied. If she ratted him out, they would be sharing a jail cell. Something that she had no desire to do. Being in the cramped apple booth had been bad enough.

183

"I remember the guy. He made a point of talking about being named after Monty Python," Jones said. "I'll keep my eye out for him and tell him to get back over here. He's probably some kind of junkie. You should be more careful, Miss Bellflower."

She snatched up three candy apples and handed them over the counter. "Don't worry about me. I'm old, but I'm wily."

Officer Jones bit a plug from his apple and walked off. The next person in line elbowed his way to the front. Camilla didn't give him much notice as she worked on another order.

"No cutting," she said absent-mindedly.

"Camilla, I need to talk to you."

It was Vince. She waved him around to the entrance of the booth. He came up behind her. She grabbed two caramel apples and handed them to a father and son. Then she moved to the next customer. Sleep would be no problem coming tonight. She had been working only two hours, but it felt like a twelve-hour workday at hard labor.

"What is it?" she asked. "I'm busy."

"Where's Graham?"

"I don't know. He got mad and stormed off." She pushed past him to get some more candied apples from a box sitting on the grass.

"How much do you know about him?"

Camilla huffed. She was far too busy to play a game of twenty questions. "Listen, if you are going to stand here flapping your gums, make yourself useful and sell some apples. I'm drowning here."

Vince nodded and stepped up to the counter. He started taking money and orders, using the placard on the tent pole to tell the price. Together they cleared the line in a few minutes. A couple of stragglers hurried up as the flurry slowed down.

"What was your question again?" she asked, remembering well what he'd said but acting like she hadn't paid much attention.

"Graham. How much do you know about him?"

"He's from California. His mom died, and he's riding across

country on his motorcycle."

"What did he do before starting his great ride?"

"We've never talked about it, but he's a good salesman and a slick talker. I guess he might have sold cars," she said.

"Do you think he might be a criminal?"

She shrugged, trying her hardest to seem nonchalant. "Maybe. I reckon anyone could be a criminal, even you."

"Could he be a murderer?"

She couldn't easily hide her surprise at the direct question. It gave her pause enough to find a response that wouldn't incriminate herself in any way. "I don't know. He's never tried to kill me. Why?"

"His motorcycle is stolen. Yesterday, I found a bunch of fake IDs in his drawer. He keeps a large serrated knife in his boot."

"Maybe he's a drug dealer. A lot of you California people are on dope, aren't you? Alabama's a good place to start up a business. We've got that methamphetamine stuff that runs rampant with the rednecks."

"I need to find him. I think it's more than that."

Vince didn't give her a chance to answer. He ran off as quickly as Graham had. Things were getting too complicated. She didn't like it at all. Camilla oftentimes felt like a spider who wove a web that suited her needs. All the complications were messing up that web. Something had to be done. If all this kept up, her cover would be blown, Tunie would complete her descent into insanity, and worst of all, she'd be alone.

Camilla turned back to the counter, ready to keep dishing out the apples. Officer Smith stood looking up at her. She didn't see his partner Officer Jones around. Smith must have gotten jealous of the apple.

"Need one of your own?" she asked, smiling and jovial.

"No ma'am." He held up a photograph of a little girl. "Have you seen her? She's missing."

Camilla took the picture and stared at it. The face looked familiar, but she'd seen lots of kids. Her age didn't help with memory either. She shook her head.

"She looks familiar, but I don't think I've seen her lately. You say she's missing?"

Officer Smith nodded his head. "Some folks say they saw her walking off with a frumpy looking guy that might have been a little slow in the head."

"I've not seen anyone like that either," she said.

"I was hoping you had. This booth gets a lot of business. Nearly everyone comes for an apple."

"They do, don't they?"

She realized what happened to the little girl. Graham had snatched her. His plan for getting her out of debt: ransom. Camilla stumbled backward and put her palm against her forehead.

"Are you okay, Miss Bellflower?" Officer Smith asked.

"A bit tired. It's been busy, and I've been working this alone." She righted herself. "I think I might close down for the night."

"You do that. We don't need you having some kind of medical emergency," Officer Smith said.

"I will."

Camilla reached out and closed the wooden flaps that covered the space above the counter. The air inside the booth stifled her. She knew that once Graham grabbed the girl, he'd go to the candy shop. He would think it was the only place that could promise complete security.

Chapter Thirty-eight

The Wasp laid the little girl down in the shed behind the Bellflower Inn. The place smelled like musty dirt and mulch. What little moonlight crept in through the cracks between the tin roof and the board walls provided him enough light to see.

The little girl didn't stir. He knew she was still alive because of her loud breathing. Sometime after slipping into the thicket behind the fairgrounds, he'd knocked her out with a blow to the back of the head. It wasn't something he'd wanted to do. No one would pay a ransom for a dead kid. For that matter, he'd never killed a girl that young. The idea felt barbaric to him, like something someone depraved would do. He was not that person. The Wasp held himself to a certain level of decency. Now she lay unconscious, and by the look of things, she would be that way for a while. He needed a chair from the house and duct tape to secure her and cover her mouth.

The Wasp slipped out of the shed and walked across the back yard to the kitchen door. No lights were on in the back of the house. That was good. He'd taken extra caution walking through the neighborhood with the little girl over his shoulder. The truck he'd stolen from a farmhouse was parked two blocks over. He'd stuck to the shadows all the way from there to the inn. Most of the town either slept or enjoyed the stupid fair.

The kitchen door creaked on its hinges. The Wasp paused and listened. Nothing moved. No one heard him. The light over the sink hummed. It cast enough light for him to search through the drawers until the found the one full of household flotsam. As he expected, he found a roll of duct tape. He took it out and grabbed a butcher knife from the block. He hated tearing duct tape with his teeth. The feel and taste of it gave him the creeps.

Sliding the roll over his hand like a bangle and sticking the knife into his back pocket, blade up, he entered the breakfast nook. The solid wood, arrow-straight chairs sat around the table.

He grabbed one and headed back to the kitchen. The swinging door from the nook to the kitchen slammed against the chair, making a loud noise. He paused and listened again. An upstairs floorboard creaked. He waited, but no one came. The Wasp sighed and returned to the yard.

As soon as his eyes adjusted to the darkness, he saw it. The door to the shed stood ajar. He'd closed it.

The Wasp put down the chair and let the roll of tape fall to the ground with a thud. He slipped the knife from his back pocket and carried it by his side, hiding it from whomever he was about to encounter. Blood lust had strangled him for days. He might get the cure for it soon. Hopefully, it wouldn't be the little girl. At this point, he might not have an option but to take care of her permanently.

As he neared the shed, he spoke in a sweet voice as if to soothe the child, "Hello."

Mary burst from the shed. He stumbled backward almost losing his footing, but kept the knife hidden. Her facial expression changed to one of horror when she recognized him.

"Why is that girl in there?" she asked.

"You didn't wake her, did you?"

"I think she's in a coma. What have you done?"

"What makes you think I did anything?"

"I saw you take her in there. What kind of monster are you?"

The Wasp smiled. He felt the grin curl his lips, like some sort of a comic book villain. Mary's expression changed again. He watched as reality dawned on her. She knew what kind of a *monster* he was. Her mouth fell open with a mixture of terror and amazement. A scream built up in her throat. He'd seen the look many times before. She squeaked when he brandished the knife, but her eyes screamed bloody murder. Now he saw that her voice was about to thaw from its icy terror.

The Wasp jabbed the blade into the soft flesh where her throat met her breast bone. It slid in with ease as if the skin were butter. The steel cut off any air heading to her larynx. The only sound that escaped from her was a pitiful high-pitch wheeze. The pain of it twisted her lips.

He withdrew the knife and jammed it into her opened mouth, embedding the tip in the back of her throat. The blade split her bottom lip. Blood poured from her wounds. It scented the night with the primal smell of gamy fear. The Wasp loved it. The fever that had built up in him raged at the scent of the stuff.

He took the knife from her mouth and started slashing. There was no pattern to his knife work. He sliced. The blade cut off her ear, sending blood spraying into the air. A cut across the side of her throat sent a jet of hot blood into the night. After his frenzy of cuts and jabs finally slowed, Mary collapsed to the ground. Her hands dug into the grass. Her breathing gurgled as blood filled her lungs. The Wasp looked at her sideways before jamming the knife into the base of her skull. The sweet sound of the vertebra popping gave him a glimmer of orgasmic pleasure.

He took a big breath. The sweet country air tinged with the ferric smell of blood intoxicated him more than any wine could. He looked down at Mary, twitching as the last nerve impulses faded away, and couldn't decide whether to leave his trademark or not. The scene would have to be cleaned. He couldn't leave her. It would lead the police to the little girl and maybe to him, definitely to the Silver Lady.

"What have you done?" Tunie yelled from behind him.

The Wasp turned and saw the old lady standing on the back stoop. Her hands covered her mouth, holding back a scream. She'd seen him. He would have to deal with her, too. It was time to find out if she was the vicious killer the Silver Lady claimed her to be.

"She kidnapped a little girl and then attacked me. I had no choice. If you don't believe me, look in the shed. You'll see the girl," he said.

Tunie looked as if she believed him. She even took one step down from the stoop. Something must have given him away, because she rallied and ran into the house. A phone hung on the wall inside the kitchen. It wouldn't take the police long to get there if she called 911.

He ran to the door. As he bounded the steps, he saw the telephone wire leading into the house. A chop with his knife sliced through it. As he walked through the door, he heard Tunie repeating "hello" from beyond the swinging door to the breakfast nook.

With the knife at his side, the Wasp took the length of the kitchen in a few wide paces. He stood on the opposite side of the door listening to Tunie's voice become more and more frantic. When the pitch in her voice hit the right place, he slammed all his weight against the door. It made solid contact with the old lady. He heard her slam into the table as the door swung free. She fell to the floor holding her stomach as he walked into the lit breakfast nook. A serrated steak knife clattered across the floor as the fall knocked it free from her hand.

"You should have looked in the shed," he said to her.

"Why?" she asked between gasps.

"Because your sister has been burying bodies out there for years. Bodies she claims you killed."

"That's a lie. I've never killed anyone," Tunie said, and then whispered so low the Wasp barely heard her. "On purpose."

The Wasp felt vicious at that moment. He wasn't sure why he wanted to reveal a secret so painful to the Silver Lady, but he did. Her piteous sister sat on the floor looking up at him with dumb eyes like some kind of child trapped in a geriatric body. Some trauma had done that to her, according to her sister. He knew better now. The Silver Lady had said that to keep her name clean if anyone ever caught on to things. Petunia Bellflower was little more than a withered magnolia blossom, like something in an old psychobiddy B-movie set in Louisiana. She was the Sweet Charlotte who needed to be hushed.

"Your sister has been killing people for their money. Poisoning them so that all three of you sisters could be together forever. She's been blaming it on you, her simple-minded baby sister. I heard what you said under your breath. There's no reason to try to protect her."

"Camilla is a good Christian woman!" Tunie said.

"She killed Lily's husband. Poisoned him," the Wasp said. "What kind of a Christian woman does that?"

"Ernie died of a heart attack!"

"What about your boyfriend?"

Tunie turned her face away. "He ran off. I wasn't good enough for him."

"He's buried somewhere your sister felt he would never be found. I'd bet he's in that shed out back," the Wasp said, "but she blamed it all on you."

"You lie." Tunie got to her feet, faster than he'd expected from the old broad.

She snatched a butter knife from the sideboard and swiped it at the Wasp. It was what he'd been waiting for. He'd needed a bit more of a catalyst to kill the old bird than her knowing what he'd done. She swung the knife like an expert. Maybe he was wrong about her murderous ways after all. This was like two gunslingers facing off in the Old West. Tunie lunged with the knife. The slightly serrated knife edge tore across his hand. It scratched more than cut, but it still hurt. He shook his head at her.

The knife sliced across her throat with a quick motion. He'd done it so many times before that his muscle had a memory for it. The old lady grabbed the gash and fell onto the table before crumpling to the floor. She would bleed out in a few moments, but she'd drawn first blood in their little affair. The Wasp would draw the last. As easy of a kill as she was, he wondered how anyone would believe she could have possibly been a vicious killer. It was laughable. The Silver Lady did not think that lie through very well.

He grabbed Tunie by the hair and pulled her head back. The knife plunged into the gash. He forced it in until the tip came out the back below her hair line. Blood slicked his hand as he let the knife handle go. Tunie fell over, dead. The Wasp almost felt sorry. It wasn't regret for killing her as much as having to hurt the Silver Lady with his actions. If he'd ever felt any true emotion of love toward someone on the planet, it was her. As he washed his hands in the kitchen sink, they trembled at the thought of her heartache. He needed to find her and tell her what he had done before someone else could. An explanation from him would make sense and soften the blow.

The Wasp walked through the house. He tracked through Tunie's blood, leaving footprints from the nook to the front door. Mary's car was gone from out front. That meant Vince was gone. That was both a good and a bad thing. He wouldn't have to deal with the man at that moment, but it would have to happen eventually. The Wasp dug the motorcycle key from his pocket as he stepped off the porch. He saw that someone had rifled through the saddlebags. Vince. The man knew who he was, and would soon find his ex-wife and Tunie dead. The Wasp would take care of Vince then. Now, he needed to find the Silver Lady.

Chapter Thirty-nine

The phone rang when Camilla walked into her shop. She locked the door and hurried to catch the call before it went to her answering machine. The message started as she snatched the receiver off the cradle.

"Hello, Camilla Bellflower," she said.

"Camilla, this is Vince." His voice sounded pressured and frightened. "I'm glad I caught you there. Are you alone?"

"Yes," she answered. "Why?"

"He's kidnapped a little girl. I found her in the shed behind your house."

"Is she alive?" Camilla asked.

Graham hacking a little girl to death would certainly complicate things, especially if he left the corpse in her shed. There were too many other skeletons in there for the police to start poking around.

"No, she's alive, but Mary's not."

"What?"

"He's killed—*mutilated* her. I think she must have caught him stowing away the little girl. Miss Bellflower, I think he might be coming for you."

A banging rattled the glass in the shop door. Camilla looked toward it. A bloodied Graham stood framed there. The greenish fluorescent lights made him look ghoulish. The frantic look on his face didn't help that appearance. She took a pad and pencil from the counter and started to write down a list of candies.

"Listen. He's here now. I'm going to have to let him in."

"You can't," Vince said. "He'll kill you."

"I don't think so." Louder banging on the door broke her concentration. "Listen, take the little girl and put her on the porch swing. I'll call 911 from here."

"You don't *think* so? You're in danger. Don't let him in!"

"I'll be fine. I need to go, or he'll suspect something."

"One more thing," Vince said. "He killed Tunie too."

Camilla looked away from the door. Tears pressed so hard in her eyes that she felt like her lids might fall off. She cleared the sob in her throat and pushed the sick feeling in her gut to her feet. So many years and deeds had been spent keeping her family together. In little more than a week, the whole thing had fallen apart. Graham banged on the door, this time making the whole frame shake. It steeled something deep inside her.

"There's a gun under the napkins in the china cabinet in the dining room. It's loaded. Get it and come here. I'll leave the door unlocked."

She hung up the phone and put the pad on the counter. With a flourish to imply that she was in a hurry, Camilla went to the door and opened it. Graham pushed his way inside. The smell of blood clung to him so strongly she thought that she might vomit on the floor.

"What took you so long?" he asked.

"I was taking an order."

He looked at her. "After hours?"

"I get a lot of calls after hours. They get left on the machine. I usually check them the next day, but I decided to write them down tonight to save time tomorrow. I'd stopped by to put my apple earnings away." She looked him over as if she'd just noticed his gory state. "What happened to you?"

"Complications."

"You didn't kill that little girl did you?"

His look this time was even more suspicious. "How do you know about her?"

"The police came around with a picture. I can put two and two together."

"She's fine, but I had to kill Mary. She saw me hiding the little brat."

"Did you bathe in her blood?" Camilla asked, trying hard to keep from slapping him in the face.

"I hit an artery. They spurt."

"What about Tunie? Did she see?"

"I don't think so. I never even saw her while I was there."

Camilla plunged her hands into the pocket of her apron to hide her clenched fists. He was a horrible liar now that she paid attention. Nothing would please her more than to slit his throat, but he was fifty years younger and far more experienced in slashing. Another gulp sent the rage back into her stomach.

"Go to the back and clean up before someone comes by and sees you. I don't have any clothes for you to change into, though."

"I'll be okay. I'll wash out my shirt and dry it in the oven for a few minutes. I'll say I had a bad nosebleed."

Graham walked into the kitchen. Camilla stood for a moment, plotting her next move. She had the opportunity to get rid of him. Vince would be there soon with the pistol. Even if he'd never used a gun before, Vince would be able to dispatch Graham. A revolver was like an old Polaroid camera, point and shoot. The problem after that was when the cops found the dead bums buried in her shed. With Tunie dead, there was no way for Camilla to prove her innocence in the murders.

"Everything okay in there?" she yelled as the water came on in the large sink.

"Where's the dish soap? You're out."

Camilla hurried to the back. Graham stood bent over the large stainless steel sink. His shirt lay folded over the bowl. The edge of the sink obscured most of his arms. An empty bottle of Joy sat on the ledge by the faucet. She walked to a cabinet well away from the food prep area. A full bottle of the yellow soap was there. She took it down and passed it over to him.

"Admiring the goods?" he asked with a big toothy smile.

"Don't be perverted. I'm your grandmother, remember?" she said, trying to hide the fact that she'd sized him up.

He scrubbed his arms down with the suds. "In name only."

Graham submerged his head under the water caught in the sink. Camilla thought about holding his head under. It was tempting, but he was too strong for her to overpower. His tight wiry torso told her that. Graham would throw up an arm, knocking her far back into the racks holding the flour and sugar.

Then she would find herself at the end of his knife blade, a place she didn't want to be.

***

The shop door opened. The Wasp barely heard it over the sound of the water splashing. He raised his head from the sink to see the Silver Lady turn toward their visitor at the storefront. He knew who it would be.

"You weren't taking an order," he said. "You called the cops."

He straightened up and shook the water from his arms. She looked nervous. Never had he expected such treachery from her. The Silver Lady should have learned from the examples he made of her sisters.

"I didn't call the cops," she said.

"Then who is it?" Another idea dawned on him. "Vince."

A wicked smile crossed his lips, one which had been there many times already that night, and it felt comfortable. It was his murderous smile, the one he got every time he was about to dispatch someone. It made him feel larger than life—*superman*.

The Wasp wheeled around to the counter and saw a wooden block full of knives within arm's length. He grabbed the biggest handle. The blade slid out with a metallic song. Music to his ears.

"Miss Bellflower?" Vince announced, as if he hadn't seen her standing in the kitchen as soon as he walked in.

By the sound of Vince's voice, he stood near the edge of the front counter. The Wasp positioned himself to the side of the door ready to swing the knife down as Vince walked into the kitchen. The Silver Lady wouldn't do anything to warn him. Even if she had called Vince, she wouldn't risk the Wasp's ire. He didn't want to harm her, but he would. She knew that. Just like he knew that if she felt it necessary, she'd kill him and blame it on her newly deceased sister.

Vince walked through the door. Without thinking, the Wasp thrust the knife down. It pierced into the man's shoulder. A scream of pain and surprise echoed through the kitchen. Vince stumbled back out the door, taking the knife with him. The Wasp grabbed another weapon. It was a paring knife. Small but deadly in his hands. He followed Vince.

"Why did you come here?" the Wasp asked. "Did she call you?"

Vince retreated to the other side of the counter. His right arm dangled limp at his side. The knife still jutted from his shoulder. He shook his head.

"I called her," he said. "I found the little girl. I found Mary and Tunie."

The Silver Lady wailed from the kitchen. It was the sound of a thousand sorrows. Despite all the rage pent up inside him, the sound almost broke the Wasp's heart. He hated that he'd given her so much of himself.

"How could you?" she cried, rushing into the room from behind him.

"She caught me," he said, without taking his eyes off of Vince. "I had no choice. If I hadn't, they would have caught us."

"Whyyyyy?" the Silver Lady wailed. "I have no one left!"

"You have me," he said.

"A lot of good that will do her," Vince said, his voice pained. "You killed her sister, my ex-wife and my daughter. Family means little to you."

The Wasp brandished the small knife. "All the killing I've done has been for family. The Silver Lady is my family."

"Silver Lady?"

"Miss Bellflower. We are family in blood. Not the kind that we share in our veins but the kind that has been on our hands."

"What are you talking about?" Vince asked, moving closer to the door.

The man's blood rolled down his arm and slicked the floor. The Wasp knew it wouldn't be long before Vince would be unable to stand, blood loss overtaking him. That's when he would make his killing move.

"I didn't kill your daughter," the Wasp said. "*She* did, for that necklace. I made it look like one of my kills because I couldn't let her take the fall. I love her too much."

"Miss Bellflower?" Vince said.

"He's lying!" she wailed. "It was Tunie! I covered up for her. I tried to tell you that days ago. She was a psychopath just like Graham."

The Wasp turned to look at the Silver Lady. Her words cut him to the soul. She hated him, and at that moment, he saw her for the pitiful old lady she was. There was no mutual love there. She would turn against him the first chance she got.

He turned back to Vince, who had drawn a snub-nosed pistol from his pocket. He aimed it at the Wasp with his left hand. It trembled from the weakness that Vince was no doubt experiencing.

The bloodlust and fury went to full steam inside the Wasp. He charged with the paring knife to slash at Vince's face and throat.

Chapter Forty

The paring blade sliced across Vince's cheek, but it stung more than anything. He fired the pistol and missed even at close range. Something shattered near him—one of the glass countertops. As Graham's little knife grazed his throat, he saw the glittering shards on the floor.

The gun popped again. He didn't even realize he'd shot. Graham stumbled backward. A red rose expanded from the killer's shoulder, and a stunned look filled his eyes. It gave Vince a newfound strength. He aimed the pistol at Graham's chest and emptied the cylinder. Two bullets missed, breaking the other counter and a jar on a shelf. The last two hit the target. Graham fell over backwards with two holes in his bare chest. Blood bubbled from them as he hit the floor. The red liquid spread across the tile mingling with Vince's own blood.

Graham drew in two ragged breathes and let out a long gurgling gasp. His eyes dulled as they stared at the ceiling. Reality came to Vince. Pain seared through his body. He could hear Miss Bellflower screaming. She walked out of the kitchen, taking in the scene.

"You did it," she said. "But look at you."

He glanced down at himself. The gun dropped from his hand, and he fell to a sitting position on the floor. Never had he killed anything, much less a human. Graham was evil, but killing another person still felt so wrong.

"Call the police," he said.

Everything started to gray out. He tottered over. Miss Bellflower hurried across and righted him before his head hit the tile. She gave him a shake. The gray faded away.

"You've got to stay conscious. I've got the thing to keep you awake."

He watched her through blurred vision as she ran to the kitchen. After what seemed like hours of banging around, she came back carrying a handful of what looked like red taffy.

"Open up. This is some strong stuff. The peppermint will rejuvenate you until help arrives."

He wasn't going to argue. A delirium fog settled over him. A little sweetness might make the difference. He didn't know. His lips parted, and he tasted the sweet, effervescent flavor of peppermint as she slid a bite-sized piece of candy into his mouth. He chewed, and the flavor seemed to revive him. His lips parted again. Miss Bellflower, tears staining her wrinkled face, pushed two more candies into his mouth. Her hand was empty now. She brushed them off on her apron. He chewed and enjoyed the sweetness.

Vince watched Miss Bellflower go to the phone. She was going to get him help. Everything was going to be okay. His mouth was full of the wonderful taste of the peppermint. It stained the edges of the growing darkness with red and white stripes like something out of a stocking on Christmas morning. Then he saw nothing.

***

Camilla hung the phone up when Vince died. She went over the story she would tell the police in her head. A well planned lie was the only way she could come out clean. They'd find all the bodies on the inn's property. With Tunie dead, she had no one to blame. Although her life would be torturous without her sisters, prison would not be in it if she had anything to say about it. She grabbed the phone and dialed 9-1-1. The operator answered.

"This is Camilla Bellflower," she screamed into the phone. "I need help! I'm at my shop. Please send help! He killed my sister and a boarder, and then he tried to kill me!"

She smiled as the operator attempted to soothe her. Things were going to work out.

Acknowledgments

I would like to thank Lauren and Laura for reading this book first, as usual. A special thanks also goes out to Matt and the folks at Pint Bottle Press. I'd also like to thank Scott Carpenter, who designed the cover for the book, and Sahara at P and G Graphics. The Blanton sisters need a nod. They inspired the Bellflowers, without the murder. The life cycle continues during the writing/publishing of a book. The case was true for one of these sisters who passed away—the oldest, Nita. I would also like to make mention of my friend and Mobile father Blake Spence, who died while I wrote this book as well. Of course, thanks to you the readers.

About the Author

Vic Kerry is the author of the novels *The Children of Lot* and *Revels Ending* and the story collection *Thorazine Dreams*. He also has short stories appearing in various anthologies and magazines. He lives in Alabama with his wife, 5 dogs, and 2 cats.

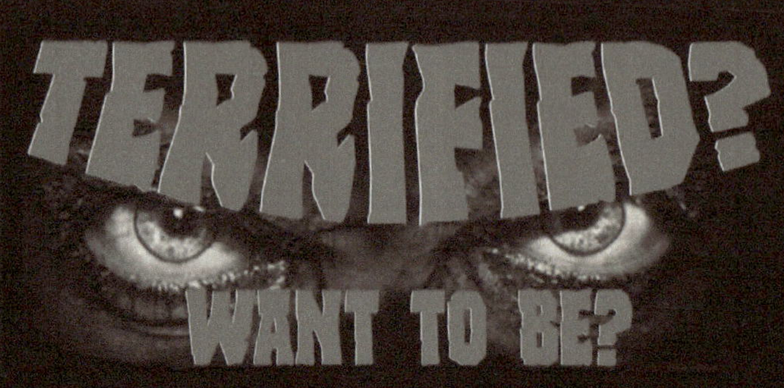

TERRIFIED?
WANT TO BE?

Thorazine Dreams
Vic Kerry
a collection

MATTHEW WEBER
A coming-of-age tale of survival
BOBCATS

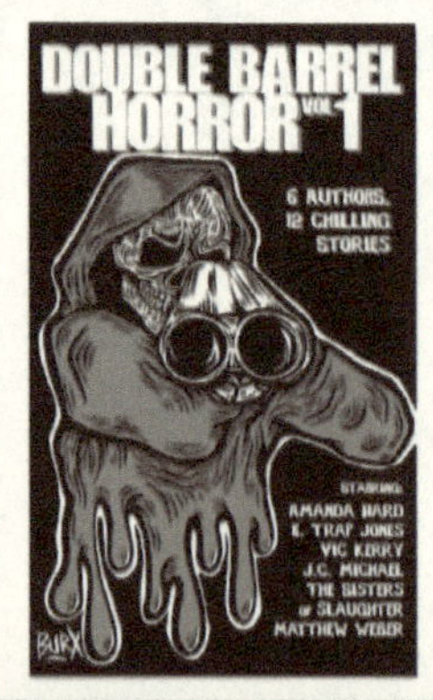

DOUBLE BARREL
HORROR VOL 1
6 AUTHORS, 12 CHILLING STORIES
STARRING
AMANDA HARD
K. TRAP JONES
VIC KERRY
J.C. MICHAEL
THE SISTERS of SLAUGHTER
MATTHEW WEBER
BURK

DOUBLE BARREL
HORROR VOL 2
12 STORIES 6 AUTHORS
STARRING
JOHN BODEN ~ SIMON DEWAR ~ PATRICK FREIVALD
CHAD LUTZKE ~ KAREN RUNGE ~ M.B. VUJACIC

www.ingramcontent.com/pod-product-compliance
Lightning Source LLC
Chambersburg PA
CBHW020809190726
48285CB00006B/2216